PRAISE FOR *LOOKER*

"It's easy to imagine that stars live gauzily perfect lives. But what happens when the illusion turns deadly? In Sims's creepy debut, a woman fixates on the actress living across the street, admiration tilting into pathology as events in her own life—infertility, her husband's desertion—unmask her fragility. The ultimate unreliable narrator, she reveals her instability slowly. By the end you'll be gasping."

—*People*

"*Looker* is a sugarcoated poison pill of psychological terror, whose wit and fluency cover its lacerating diagnosis of the deranging effects of envy, perhaps the most widespread social sickness of our age. The novel disturbs because we are all, to some degree, susceptible to the bacillus of the narrator's insanity. And her symptoms may be more recognizable than we care to admit."

—*The Wall Street Journal*

"A wicked slow-burn . . . *Looker* glides toward its ending as if eagerly awaiting the discovery of something ghastly."

—*Entertainment Weekly*

"In prose that moves between lyrical and caterwauling, the poet Laura Sims has pulled off the high-wire act of making bitterness delicious."

—*Vogue*

"In the end, the Hitchcockian thrills of *Looker* prove only skin-deep; the book unmasks itself as a twisted portrait of pain. . . . *Looker*, at a hundred and eighty pages, lasts about as long as a movie, and not even half as long as a full night's sleep. It's an ephemeral fiction with a hard landing—like a window, seen in passing, that glows and goes dark."

—*The New Yorker*

"Is *Looker* a warning? A character study? An exploration of grief? A critique of American culture? It is all of these things, as well as a novel about what it means to be seen—and what it means to be unseen. Most essentially, it is a heady thriller that asks a reader to engage with a narrator who has been told by circumstance that she has nothing to live for, and who fills the empty spaces in her life with an unhealthy obsession. *Looker* demands the reader look at—really gaze at, live with, and experience—dangerous obsession, but more pointedly, the societal expectations that might lead to it in the first place."

—*Ploughshares*

"A spectacular debut novel . . . Her narrator's stunning descent takes her deep into darkness, and Sims's masterful ending caps a book which does everything right."

—*The Star-Ledger*

"This debut is a penetrating and unsettling psychological thriller. . . . It's a novel about identity, appearances, and envy, and it's one of the season's most timely reads, an innovative experiment in what a thriller can be."

—*CrimeReads*

"In this electrifying Hitchcockian debut, an unhappy woman's obsession with a nearby actress will push the boundaries between insanity and desperation."

—*Washington Independent Review of Books*

"*Looker* is a powerful sylph of a book about creation and destruction and the permeable boundary between them."

—*Literary Hub*

"Tense, twisted, and briskly paced, poet Laura Sims's debut novel, *Looker*, is the progressively disturbing story of one woman's grief-fueled spiral downward to an irredeemable rock-bottom. . . . Somewhat surprisingly, the most disturbing thing about *Looker* is the creeping sense of complicity that Sims engenders in the reader. . . . By the end, Sims compels us to ask: Have we been deranged, predatory voyeurs into the actress's life—or into the narrator's?"

—*Shelf Awareness*

"I've said it before and I'll say it again, I can't wait to see *Looker* on the big (or small) screen one day. . . . If you loved *The Woman in the Window* or *Girl on the Train*, you won't be able to put Laura Sims's book down."

—Women.com

"Laura Sims's sharp debut novel is a thriller about an unhealthy fixation between neighbors, one that's propelled by the unnamed narrator's unraveling as she descends into a vortex of resentment and obsession."

—*Southern Living*

"Jealousy rears its ugly head in Sims's chilling and riveting debut. In this tightly plotted novel, Sims takes the reader fully into the mind of a woman becoming increasingly unhinged, and turns her emotionally fraught journey into a provocative tale about the dangers of coveting what belongs to another."

—*Publishers Weekly* (starred review)

"Like a modern-day version of Poe's "The Tell-Tale Heart," Sims's novel shows the warped reality and claustrophobic mentality of a person losing a grip on her moral compass. . . . [With] original and electric moments . . . this novel gallops along at top speed."

—*Kirkus Reviews*

"Readers fond of protagonists who profess to guzzling wine

at nine a.m. will breeze right through this one's bad decisions, moments of shocking clarity and cruelty, and—no spoilers!—total undoing. A dark and stylish drama featuring a self-aware yet unstable narrator."

—*Booklist*

"[A] gripping and intense debut . . . This twisted and tightly coiled tale will define obsession on a new level."

—*Library Journal*

"A perfect, dark pleasure . . . propelled by a woman whose obsession with a famous actress spurs one irredeemable trespass after another. A rare debut filled with gorgeous sentences, savory twists, and shot through with ferocious truths, this is the kind of book that can only be written by an author who is thrillingly unafraid."

—Mona Awad, author of *Bunny*

"Sims's debut is a breathless and unrelenting portrait of one woman's unraveling."

—Greer Hendricks, *New York Times* bestselling coauthor of *The Wife Between Us*

"With an agile precision reminiscent of Lydia Davis, Laura Sims captures the obsessiveness of a woman who unravels after the collapse of her marriage. A taut, gripping portrait, all the more sinister for its elegance."

—Leni Zumas, author of *Red Clocks*

"Like Polanski's *Repulsion*, Laura Sims's intense, gripping first novel shoehorns us into a gathering sense of dread, heightened at every turn by our sympathy for her relentlessly unraveling protagonist. The precise, observant writing slips through the skin without ever calling attention to itself."

—Peter Straub, author of *A Dark Matter* and *Interior Darkness*

LOOKER

A NOVEL

LAURA SIMS

SCRIBNER

NEW YORK LONDON TORONTO SYDNEY NEW DELHI

Scribner
An Imprint of Simon & Schuster, Inc.
1230 Avenue of the Americas
New York, NY 10020

This book is a work of fiction. Any references to historical events, real
people, or real places are used fictitiously. Other names, characters, places,
and events are products of the author's imagination, and any resemblance to
actual events or places or persons, living or dead, is entirely coincidental.

Copyright © 2019 by Laura Sims

All rights reserved, including the right to reproduce this book
or portions thereof in any form whatsoever. For information, address
Scribner Subsidiary Rights Department,
1230 Avenue of the Americas, New York, NY 10020.

First Scribner trade paperback edition October 2019

SCRIBNER and design are registered trademarks of The Gale Group, Inc.,
used under license by Simon & Schuster, Inc., the publisher of this work.

For information about special discounts for bulk purchases,
please contact Simon & Schuster Special Sales at 1-866-506-1949
or business@simonandschuster.com

The Simon & Schuster Speakers Bureau can bring authors
to your live event. For more information or to book an event,
contact the Simon & Schuster Speakers Bureau at
1-866-248-3049 or visit our website at www.simonspeakers.com.

Interior design by Kyle Kabel

Manufactured in the United States of America

1   3   5   7   9   10   8   6   4   2

Library of Congress Cataloging-in-Publication Data is available.

ISBN 978-1-5011-9911-0
ISBN 978-1-5011-9912-7 (pbk)
ISBN 978-1-5011-9913-4 (ebook)

For Margaret Lewis

t was Mrs. H who started calling her *the actress*, making it sound like she was one of those old Hollywood legends—Audrey Hepburn, Grace Kelly, Lauren Bacall. That may have been accurate early in her career, when she was a serious indie star, but now her fiercely sculpted, electric-blue-clad body adorns the side of nearly every city bus I see. It's an ad for one of those stupid blockbusters—and she isn't even the *main* star, she's only the *female* star—so she's a sellout, like all the rest. It's disappointing only because she belongs to us. To our block, I mean.

And here she comes—passing so close to where I sit on my stoop that I can see the tiny blue bunny rabbits embroidered on her baby's hat. She has him strapped to her chest in that cloth contraption all the moms have. It should look ludicrous, the baby an awkward lump on the front of her white linen sundress, but somehow the actress pulls it off. She more than pulls it off—as he peers up at her she lowers her head and shakes her shoulder-length auburn hair in his face. He squeals in delight. They look like they're being filmed right now, like they're co-starring in a shampoo commercial,

1

but there's only me watching. She knows I'm sitting here but she doesn't acknowledge me when she passes by. She just stares straight ahead with that slight smile, meant to be mysterious, I'm sure. *I see your airbrushed body on the bus almost every day!* I want to call out. I take a long drag on my cigarette and blow a cloud of smoke after her and the babe.

*

Later on, riding the subway home after my night class, I wonder about the sad sacks filling my train car. What are their twelve-hour workdays like? Full of tedium and sullen acceptance? Rage? The women's faces have gone slack and gray by this time of night. The men's shirts are rumpled, with sweat stains at the pits. A few reek of cigarettes and booze. There they sit, swaying and bumping in the unclean air. Does the actress ever take the subway? Maybe once in a while, to prove that she's a regular person. But usually there's a car outside her house, idling, waiting to whisk her anywhere she wants or needs to go. "To the park," I imagine her saying. To the theater, to the trendy restaurant I've never heard of, to the Apple Store, to the apple orchard upstate. Meanwhile I sit on the stoop or shrug myself up, back and legs aching, to find my greasy MetroCard and join the tide of commoners underground. Does she remember how hot it is down on the platform in late summer? And how cold it gets in winter? Until you step inside the train car and have to struggle out of your heavy coat and scarf (if you can, packed as you are like sardines) because it's steaming and suddenly so are you. Does she remember these and other indignities of "regular person" city life? Does she breathe a sigh of relief every time she passes one of the station entrances in her sleek black car? I would. I'm certain I would. The past would seem like a distant bad dream. Or a joke.

I pass by the actress's house on my way home, as usual. A rich yellow glow spills from the garden-level windows of her brownstone. I've never seen a prettier, more welcoming room in all my life. The hardwood floor, the stainless steel appliances, and the wood-topped island at the heart of the kitchen all gleam under the yellow light. Closer to the window, there's a cozy play area with expensive-looking toys strewn across a simple beige carpet. Wooden animals, an elaborate dollhouse, a riding toy for the baby. Only the best for her three kids. Only the handmade, the safest, the locally sourced, the organically grown. In that, she and her husband are no different from everyone else around here, coddling their children with overpriced toys, clothes, and food—and then the kids will grow up hating their parents anyway, just like the ones raised on spankings, secondhand smoke, and Oscar Mayer lunch meats do.

Tonight, the husband leans on the kitchen island, chatting comfortably with the cook as she works. The husband is a screenwriter—that's how he and the actress met, he co-wrote one of her earliest films. He's handsome, of course—Iranian American, with shining dark eyes and a lush but neatly trimmed black beard. Now *that's* a beard. Not like the straggly hipster beards you see around here. The husband could be a movie star himself, but he remains a writer. Happy to be in her shadow, I suppose. Or not happy, merely biding his time before he leaves her for the nanny . . . or the cook? Either would be a very poor choice, considering what he'd be leaving behind. The two girls are seated in the play area, organizing the dollhouse. Bickering, I think. The eight-year-old girl, an exact replica of the actress, with her auburn hair and wide-set green eyes, brushes the six-year-old's hand away from a minuscule wardrobe, and then moves it herself. The younger sister pouts, folding her arms over her chest and glaring at the back of her sister's head. She has her father's dark hair and dark eyes. The two of them look like cousins rather than sisters. The black-haired, green-eyed baby, though, is a perfect mix of his parents' genes; he sits behind the girls, chewing placidly on some sort of squeezy toy shaped like a giraffe.

The actress sits alone at the kitchen table in the back of the room with her face lighted by her laptop screen, typing away at something—an e-mail? A novel? A tweet to her followers and fans? I know she tweets—or someone tweets *for* her—but she isn't very active on Twitter. She mostly retweets women's rights activists, left-leaning politicians, and her famous friends. I tried following her on Instagram once, thinking I'd get a window into her innermost life, but it was just a carefully managed picture parade. Magazine-style shots of things like fresh blueberries heaped in a child's hand (#summer!), the sunset from an airplane window (#cominghomeatlast), one artfully blurred, close-up "selfie" of her and her husband's faces (#datenight). Maybe it wasn't a curated account, maybe it really was her posting, but I knew I wouldn't find any intimate moments there that could match what I saw through her window almost daily.

A full glass of wine sits by her hand. *Too close,* I want to say. I lean toward the window. *You should move that wine away from your laptop—I lost one that way, once.* But nothing will happen to the actress's laptop: she won't spill the wine, and even if she does, won't she just laugh as a staff member mops up the mess and sets a gleaming new computer before her? And then continue as she was, typing merrily away, completely unscathed?

I've never crossed their little fenced-in garden, of course. I stand on the sidewalk in front of the fern-and-ivy-filled

planter that hangs from the fence—placed there as a sort
of screen, I'm sure—and have a direct line of view into
the kitchen at night. I'm grateful they've never thought to
install blinds. That's how confident they are. *No one would
dare stand in front of our house and watch us*, they think. And
they're probably right: except for me.

People pass behind me, probably mistaking me for the
actress, the golden one relaxing for a moment in the cool
night air. *Was that her?* they wonder. But they don't turn
back to look—it would be too intrusive. Sometimes I even
pretend to be her when someone walks by. I straighten up
a bit, try to hold my head at that particular angle she does,
try to act like I've just stepped away from my arduous,
exalted life. By the time I've made this transformation in
posture and attitude, they're already gone, and it's just me,
alone at the gate.

In *The Sultan of Hanover Street*, a moody indie film from ten
years ago, she played the adult daughter of the star, Rich-
ard McKane, who looked fifty though he was surely in his
seventies by then. She proved herself in *Sultan*, especially
in the hospital scene. She played it straight, without tears
or cheap sentimentality. She was captivating. I remember
sitting in the dark next to Nathan, studying her face for
the first time: the sharp cheekbones and those giant green

eyes. Her features loomed large, unbearably beautiful, as though she belonged to some glorious alien race. I fixed my inferior eyes on that face and felt it lift me out of my seat, out of my life for a moment. The warmth of Nathan's hand in mine brought me back, held me down, made me thankful to be exactly where and who I was.

Nathan. That hand is gone, and has taken him with it. Or vice versa. Whatever. He's gone.

So she gathered her accolades for the role in *Sultan*—not an Oscar, but a Golden Globe for Best Supporting Actress and glowing reviews. She did more indie work for a while, spreading her roots through the Hollywood soil, building her rep as an indie darling, and then? She sold. Right. Out. She signed on to do a Michael Bay movie—something with a tsunami and killer robots. What a joke. But it was a huge hit with the masses and it made her famous. She promptly married her screenwriter boyfriend, bought her house here, and started having babies. Her first two came the standard two years apart—the boy an unconventional five-plus years later. What happened in the intervening years? Fertility issues like mine? Marital trouble? Or was the third child one of those "happy accidents"? Maybe it was none of the above. Maybe one day she woke up, hungering for another baby, and so she went and had one—just like that. I wonder if she'll stop at three. Why should she, with others to do the messy work? I see her with the kids, but rarely with more than one at a time. The other moms in this neighborhood teeming with families pile their strollers with two, even three kids at once, struggling and cursing under their breaths as they push uphill toward the park. But the actress makes parenting look glamorous and fun. She's always stylishly dressed, even in weekend clothes, and I can't imagine her breaking a sweat. If I were a local mom, I would hate her. *It isn't as easy as you make it look!* I would shout through her ground-floor windows. Imagine how my voice would pierce the cozy domestic scene! The kids would run to the windows, hands and faces pressed to the glass. The baby might burst into tears. The husband would furrow his handsome brow and start immediately for the door. *Who goes there?* I imagine him calling into the night. And the actress? She'd glance up for a moment with a distant, distracted smile, take a sip from her wineglass, and go back to her screen.

*

The actress's baby is screaming his head off in front of my building. The nanny, a skinny strawberry blonde, leans her head close to his in the stroller and shushes him gently, waving a toy in his face and letting him grab it. He continues to scream. She rummages in the diaper bag slung across the stroller handles and then sighs. Finally she notices me, smoking on the front stoop, just a few feet away. We've exchanged smiles and brief greetings over the past months, whenever she's passed by with the stroller. Once, I got up the nerve to say, "Cute boy," and she replied, "Yes, but he's a handful," in a cheerful, maternal way. I fought the urge to ask if the baby was hers—knowing, of course, that it wasn't—but hoping it would prompt her to share some tidbit about her boss. Even to hear her say the actress's name would have given me a little thrill. "I've left his pacifier at home," she says now. "Oh no," I say, frowning sympathetically. The child's screams seem to crescendo at the word *pacifier*. The nanny starts to turn around for home with him, shaking her head, when I stand abruptly and say, "Wait." She looks up at me, takes in the cigarette still smoking in my hand. I drop it, crush it under my heel, and go down the steps to her. "I'll watch him for a minute while you run back. It's no trouble, really." She starts to protest; I can see her weighing the convenience of going back without the cumbersome stroller versus the potential anger of her employers if they were to find out. "I don't mind a screaming little one," I say, looking her in the eye and placing a hand on her arm. "They live so close. It will only take you a second, right?" She glances back at her employer's house—ten, fifteen steps away, tops!—then looks back at me. "Right," she says. "Thank you. I won't be a minute." And she speed-walks down the block. So here I am, alone with the actress's baby. He may be red-faced and screaming, but he is all mine. So delicious, waving his little arms in the air, arching his back against the straps that hold him in. I kneel down in front of him and wriggle my fingers in front of his face, making clucking noises with my tongue. He stares at me and screams even louder, writhes all the more powerfully in his seat. The poor thing! I start to unbuckle him. I will hold him to me, smell his head, brush my lips over his downy hair. But the damn buckles are so complicated, and before I can get him out, the nanny materializes beside me. She pops the pacifier in his mouth, thanks me profusely, and pushes the stroller along up the street.

Just like that, he's gone. Gone like Nathan. Gone like the baby we never had. I drag myself back up the steps and inside.

Upstairs, everything's a mess. The cat—the damn cat, Nathan's cat—has tracked her litter through the kitchen again. I had the leak beneath the sink fixed days ago, but the cabinet still reeks of mildew. Romantic brownstone living! Trash piled in the can, dirty laundry piled in the hamper. Nathan used to do all that—clean up after the cat, take out the trash, take care of the laundry. I try to keep up but I've been barely functional since he left.

I'm not alone, though, I tell myself: I have my books. My student papers to grade. My students, I suppose. I have my colleagues at school, too—a few, at least, who aren't self-important jerks, lecherous drunks, or socially awkward weirdos. Or all of those rolled into one (which would make: my department chair). I also have two or three old friends, one of whom I see regularly for lunch. That's the sum total of my life, since Nathan left six weeks ago. Oh, and Cat, the stupid cat that Nathan's had since grad school . . . who's now been abandoned just like me. Here we are, unlikely pair in misery, doing our best to stay out of each other's way. I feed her to keep her alive—that's it.

*

I walk past the actress on my way home from the grocery store. Our eyes meet for a moment, then she looks away. *You're ugly*, I think. Without meaning to. But it's true—at least today, in this afternoon light, she looks too raw, too hugely featured. Her eyes bulge, her lips are almost obscenely plush, and her cheekbones jut beneath her thin skin. In the mirror at home, I push my fingers around my face. Small nose, thin lips, and nearly invisible cheekbones. But I've got fairy-tale eyes—bright blue, almond shaped. When the actress looked at me today, maybe she thought: *You should be on the screen.* Maybe that's why she had to look away.

We've spoken only once, at last year's block party. The neighborhood kids—including her two girls—were thrashing around inside the net walls of the bouncy house. Grown-ups were gathered in loose circles nearby, sitting on folding chairs or standing, chatting aimlessly, pleased by the excuse to drink beer at noon. I was standing in front of our house with my dish of watermelon and feta orzo salad in hand, waiting for Nathan to come down, when I saw her from the corner of my eye. She walked over to the food table, holding a bag from City Pantry, a gourmet food and kitchen gadgets shop new to the neighborhood. I made a beeline for the table, brandishing my dish. I flashed her a smile. Our eyes met. "Where's that?" I blurted out, pointing at her bag. "What?" she said in her famously husky voice. "Oh. City Pantry. It's just two blocks from here. Delicious stuff." I nodded, watching her unload container after container of costly gourmet sides: Parmesan roasted acorn squash, portobello mushrooms sautéed in wine, grilled shrimp and octopus salad, braised bacon-wrapped endives—dishes it would take all day for some ragged woman like me to cook. I scrambled to think of what to say next, how to keep her there with me. "Looks good!" I said at last, hating what must be the desperate-looking grin on my face. But she smiled back, generous soul, and then floated away in her ankle-length burnt-orange sundress and floppy straw hat, back to her beautiful house. I watched her go, feeling melted inside. Like I'd been touched by the warm, immense hand of a goddess. When the feeling left a few moments later, shame replaced it. It crept up my neck in a hot flush. What had I said? "Looks good!" Like some half-wit. Some rube.

I'm interesting! I wanted to shout. *I'm somebody, too!* But then Nathan was beside me, slipping his arm around my waist, and the self-loathing dropped away. After an hour of chatting with neighbors, Nathan at my side, I'd forgotten the whole stupid scene. Well, not the scene, but at least I'd let go of the deep humiliation. I barely turned my head, later, when the actress reappeared, radiant and cool as ever. I could be immune to her sometimes, back then.

There's a scene in the actress's second movie, *Girl with Dog,* an earnest indie rom-com, where she tells her friend, "Love makes you interesting. It makes *everyone* interesting." She delivers the line with such gusto, her green eyes bright and even slightly moist. The friend scoffs and says, "Yeah, right. Everyone but me."

*

Today I decide to throw out all the meds. The Gonal, the Menopur, the Ganirelix Acetate—what *was* all that stuff I was injecting into my body? Hundreds of dollars' worth of chemical compounds meant to make my defective eggs perform correctly for once, that's what. After drinking my coffee-only breakfast, I dump it all in a giant black trash bag: the boxes of prefilled syringes and sterile pads and Band-Aids and alcohol wipes, and their bland, insulting optimism with them. I tie a knot at the top of the bag and carry it downstairs to toss in the bin. I hesitate for a second on the stoop. I could keep the stuff a little longer, in the hopes of finding someone new to drag through the same torturous cycle of hope, elation—our hands clasping and eyes meeting as the doctor describes how beautifully the embryo transfer went—followed by the toxic letdown of "Not Pregnant" appearing in the window of one of those damn expensive digital pee-sticks. Or I could leave the bag on the street for some other deficiently wombed woman—although from the looks of it around here, everyone but me is doing fine in that department. So forget it. The bag of meds goes in the trash. I'm done.

It feels good. Clean. Empty—like my womb. Ha.

The first appointment at the fertility clinic was the best. Nathan and I had found our solution—hooray! We sat, hands clasped in front of Dr. J, nodding our heads in unison at the test results, as if saying, *She understands us, she understands our needs!* And she did. Or so we thought. I spent hours of my life in that waiting room, and in the countless exam rooms the nurses would usher me into—to be weighed, measured, probed, and sometimes inseminated. I kept up a positive attitude for as long as I possibly could—making jokes with the doctor and nurses, offering up my veins to them and willingly splaying my legs. Eventually, all of our savings went down the drain. My marriage, too, though that drained away at a more leisurely pace. And I can't blame it all on the cost and complexity of fertility treatments, can I? Or even on my—no, *our*, the doctor emphasized, but come on, it was *my*—infertility. Nathan was tested and his sperm was "perfect." It wasn't him, it was *me*. Dr. J herself grew increasingly cold with me as the weeks and months passed. Like I must be one of those *bad* patients, like I must be failing repeatedly on purpose. It wasn't fair—and yet I understood her disgust. I felt it, too.

I went to yoga religiously back in those days. I remember feeling cleansed and purified after the intense hour and a half. Hopeful and hearty. Willowy and strong. Full of Buddhist platitudes and a sense of peace. I tried to keep going in the days after Nathan left, I tried to "clear my mind" and "open my heart" as the instructor suggested, but I was revolted by the stifling room and the stink of other people's sweat—and, most of all, by my yoga instructor's wish for "peace everywhere." *What about peace here? What about me?* I raged inside.

Just the other day, Mrs. H said, "Where's your husband?" I stared at her. *Where's yours?* I wanted to say back. *Dead and buried*, she would have had to answer. I envy her that clear resolution. Better to be left for death than for . . . nothing at all, not even another woman! Better to have Nathan snug under the ground than out walking the world without me.

*

I wake with a heavy sludge in my stomach. I dreamed of Nathan last night. He was lost in a crowd of strangers, and I was pushing through the throng to reach him, screaming his name, seeing what I thought was the top of his head just a few feet in front of me. Always out of reach. I woke to nothingness. Dumb cat purring beside me in what used to be Nathan's spot. My eyes itch just looking at her. I smack my hand down on the comforter and watch the cat rear back. But then she calms, and resettles, as if nothing has happened. As if I'm no one, nothing at all.

*

Nathan and I moved here to be near the park, for our imaginary future brood. Five years later, here I sit, still strategically, uselessly close to the park. I haven't been there in weeks. Months, maybe. What's there for me? *You should exercise more*, Nathan would say, sweat beading his brow after his early morning run around the park's central loop. I'd glare at him over my second cup of coffee. *I'm movie-star thin*, I'd say. *That isn't the point*, he'd counter. And so it went.

Kale shakes. Blueberry-and-banana smoothies, with ginger tossed in. Wheatgrass shots. Hold the bun, please. Gluten-free chips or pretzels. Gluten-free bread. Gluten-free . . . whateverthefuck. Our pantry could have stocked a natural foods shop. I think he thought surely it would rub off on me one day. Especially when the rounds of IVF continued to be unsuccessful. *We should try everything, right?* he'd say, meaning *you* should try everything, waving one of his damn smoothies in my face. *Fuck off*, I'd reply. Did he really think kale would get "us" pregnant? I was constantly moving his organic crap to the back of the fridge so I could make room for my Diet Cokes and cream cheese.

I thought up ways to murder him, when we fought. I thought I could smother him in his sleep, or lace his kale smoothie with something untraceable, blame his early death on a (nonexistent) congenital heart condition. *I was always afraid this would happen*, I'd say to the police, wringing my hands. There was one bad blowup we had, when I wanted to take a break, let a few months pass between IVF cycles. This was after several failed cycles in a row, and I felt exhausted by the unending clinic visits followed by the vicious little needle pricks at home, all leading to: zero. Nathan was supposed to be helping—he'd been all too eager to do the injections in the beginning—but as we both gradually lost heart, he left it all to me. There I sat, stabbing my belly and thigh. Alternating between the left and right sides every day. Feeling the medicine burn as it spread, gritting my teeth against the pain. And yet *he* despised the idea of my taking a break! Said we couldn't afford to let any time pass, given "the state of your eggs." Accused me of being selfish, negligent, indifferent. I screamed at him that I wanted to rip his head off. And I did want to: I imagined doing it, in graphic detail, after he'd stormed out of the apartment. When he came back we made up, as usual, though each blowup brought us one baby step (ha!) closer to the end.

*

Nathan and I moved into our apartment at the same time another couple moved into the duplex downstairs. Dillon, the husband, was a software engineer, and Farrah, the wife, worked in pharmaceutical advertising. They were one of the new breed infesting our neighborhood: generic rich folk. I despised them in general but liked them in particular—or tolerated them, anyway. We made a few empty gestures toward getting together, having a drink at one of our places, going out for brunch, but it never materialized. We had our lives; they had theirs. They were always friendly, smiling, and helpful when something went wrong in the building. Then Farrah got pregnant, right in the middle of our baby-making hell.

It was bad enough that I had to watch her huffing up and down the stairs, holding—no, clutching!—the rail like the sanctified vessel she was, carrying what must feel like the world's most precious cargo as her belly grew and grew. But her personality changed, too. She started to send me frosty texts about things in the building that bothered her, especially as she feathered her nest. *Could you or Nathan sweep the stoop once in a while? I've had to do it twice this week.* Or: *Would you move those air-conditioning units out of the downstairs hallway? We'll need to store our stroller there,* she'd write, without preamble of any kind, not even a *Hi!* At first I was accommodating, writing back a cheery *Sure!* And sending Nathan down to do her bidding. But then I'd go upstairs and jab myself with a needle full of some hormone that would give me insomnia and no babies. No babies no babies no babies. She'd done it effortlessly, she and her husband, at least as far as I knew: he'd stuck his dick in her, the sperm had met the right egg, and presto! The way God intended it. Not this artificial way we were going about things. I thought, too, that Farrah had begun to look at me askance for my blatant unpregnantness. Nathan told me I was imagining it—of course he did! And of course he was right, I agreed, although inside I knew differently. So when her texts grew more and more passive-aggressive, I decided to strike back with passive aggression of my own. I used silence: whenever she sent one of her obnoxious requests, I simply didn't respond. Nathan would sigh, shake his head, and tell me to "be reasonable." Did Farrah's husband, the mild-mannered engineer, tell her the same? *Be reasonable, Farrah, they probably can't have kids. Have pity on her.* But I didn't *want* her damn pity. And as far as I could tell, she wasn't offering it. The looks she gave me weren't sympathetic; they were disapproving. *Why can't she have kids?* they seemed to ask. *What's wrong with her?*

One day, late in her pregnancy, I ran into Farrah in our shared front garden. Rather than her usual scowl, she beamed a brilliant, toothy smile my way and I saw the old her, the charming brunette with the deep brown eyes who got whatever she wanted, including that massive belly. I couldn't help responding in kind. I smiled back. "Have you heard of Virtual Doorman?" she asked, almost glee-fully. "No," I said, instantly on guard. Our doorbell had never worked reliably—sometimes it buzzed, sometimes it didn't—so Farrah and Dillon had to sign for our packages now and then. As her due date drew nearer, she seemed to find this arrangement increasingly intolerable. *Had to sign for a package while you were out,* she'd text. *I was in the shower when they rang.* I'd grit my teeth and write nothing in return. "It's a service you can install that answers the door when you're out," she said now, in an excited rush. "It can even let deliv-erymen in to drop packages in the downstairs hall. I think it might be just the thing!" Of course. That explained her sudden upward mood swing. "Oh!" I said, matching her tone. "That's great, we'll definitely look into it!" Then I gave her a friendly wave. I promptly forgot about the stupid Virtual Doorman, even after she'd texted me the link to the site.

Fast-forward to two weeks later: Nathan and I were out in the city one Saturday, exploring the waterfront area, holding hands and sipping coffee and feeling positive that this time, this round of IVF had worked. I felt preg-nant-ish, I thought. For sure. My boobs were sore, and my very punctual period was at least a day late. Nathan was so inspired that he'd begun doing the injections for me again. All was well. Then my phone dinged with a text from Farrah. *Just had to sign for another package of yours. Have you ordered the Virtual Doorman yet??* it said. I felt remarkably calm. She couldn't rattle me, not then. I showed the text to Nathan, who raised his eyebrows as if he could finally see what I'd been saying about her. "You should just say NO, in all caps," he suggested, and we laughed. So I wrote, *NO.* And a moment later my phone dinged again, like she'd been staring at her screen just waiting for a snarky reply. *Why not?* her text said. It felt like we were circling each other, fists raised, flinging insults, even though neither of us had said anything remotely insulting. *Because I'm busy,* I wrote, knowing that Farrah had just quit her job to stay home with the baby. *Some of us have work to do,* I added. When Nathan read my text, he looked playfully shocked. We high-fived—blissful, triumphant team members that we were. *We won!* I kept thinking all day. Until late at night, when my period came.

Nathan went behind my back and ordered the damn Virtual Doorman, as if we needed a remote service answering our door—as if we could afford it! When I confronted him about it, he shrugged his shoulders to say, *It was fun being on your team while it lasted.* I could sense Farrah's smug satisfaction from two floors up. Is that when things between Nathan and me really began to fray? Or had it already begun, and this just accelerated our undoing?

I watched Farrah's belly grow bigger and bigger, watched her move more and more slowly up the stoop. Meanwhile, I'd gone through two consecutive egg harvestings, a promising embryo transfer, and two weeks later: zip. I'd crammed a whole pineapple down my throat, like all the blogs said to do after IVF, and rested, and taken my folic acid, and still the squirming little life, the tiny light they'd shown me on the ultrasound screen during the procedure, had winked out and died. Why hadn't those slimy progesterone suppositories I'd stuck up me three times a day made my womb hospitable? Why did nothing ever work? Dr. J was reserved in offering her condolences this time; she pursed her lips. "Have you thought about trying acupuncture, too?" she asked. I had no intention of submitting to even *more* needles—I'd had enough of them, and so had my bruised belly—but I didn't say that, I just said I'd think about it. I always said I'd think about it. Telling Nathan the news was difficult, but he swallowed his disappointment and comforted me, told me we'd try again and it would work next time, blah blah blah. I didn't believe it as he said it, and I certainly don't believe it now, knowing he was probably beginning to plan his escape by then.

When the baby came—Farrah's baby—she started making a habit of leaving trash bags filled with dirty diapers outside

her door, presumably for Dillon to take out when he got
home from work. I couldn't believe it! Ms. Perfect, Ms.
Persnickety! It wasn't too bad at first, but as the baby grew,
his shits started to reek. Jesus. I'd come home midday and it
would hit me like a hot, wet, horrible wall: that sickly-sweet,
unmistakable odor. *Do you smell that?* I'd ask Nathan. He'd
look up distractedly. *What?* As if he lived in a different
building, on a different plane. As if it were *me* who stunk,
not the precious baby's poop. I started carrying the bags
out to the trash. Day after day I did this, and day after day
I waited for the text from her that would say, *Thank you,
I'm sorry for the smell.* Or *Forgive my laziness and rudeness—you're
a lifesaver.* Or *How would I get by without you, neighbor?* I would
show it to Nathan and he'd see what a necessary angel I
was. Needless to say, the text never came. Eventually Farrah
just stopped putting trash bags in the hall, and that was
the end of that.

Farrah and Dillon moved out just after Nathan left. She
was hugely pregnant with their second child; I was dragging
myself around like the newly risen dead. "We've outgrown
the place," Dillon said cheerfully, when I ran into him one
day on the stoop and plastered a smile on my face to distract
him from my red-rimmed, puffy eyes. They'd be moving
to a condo in the city, he said. A spacious, three-bedroom,
two-bath overlooking the river. They'd go on to have a

whole brood, I was sure—like everyone else in this place. The more kids you had, the more prosperous it meant you were. Meanwhile there I sat on the stoop: zero kids, zero husband, a woman-shaped shade. Haunting an apartment that was empty except for my ex-husband's cat.

I despised Dillon and Farrah, but their absence made the house feel even emptier. There seemed to be no sign of new people coming to fill the vacant duplex, either, which was weird, given the cutthroat rental market around here. There were always new suckers to lure in, people willing or desperate enough to pay an extraordinary amount of money for a small set of rooms they could run through like rats. But nothing. No one. I'd begun to suspect that Charles, our absentee landlord, who had raised his children here and then fled to Miami in retirement, was planning to sell the building. He'd bought the place for peanuts years ago, and now he could sell it for $3 million at least. I imagined he was waiting me out. Last time our lease had come up, Nathan had negotiated a discount in exchange for paying a year's worth of rent in advance—clever man. Now I worried that Charles would kick me out in March, when the lease expired. I could e-mail and ask him point-blank if he planned to sell, of course, and at least resolve the anxiety of not knowing, but I didn't want to draw attention to the situation. As if asking him might give him the idea to sell, if he didn't have it already. I stayed silent and tried not to think about it—about what I would do or where I would go when the building sold or the money ran out. Next March was still months away.

*

Coffee mug in hand, I watch the actress from three stories up. She holds her baby loosely on her hip and walks at a leisurely pace. She smiles down at him, says something, *goo goo ga ga*, for all I know, and laughs at whatever sounds he makes in response. She seems completely relaxed, her smile real. Not the tight one she's given me when I've passed her on the street. Not the diamond-bright one she gives the cameras. She's wearing that same boho-chic white linen sundress I've seen before—it's deceptively simple but surely expensive. The whiteness shows off her lightly tanned skin, gleaming from whatever weekend beach trip they must have taken recently. The baby waves his arms and squirms against her, so she cuddles him closer, kissing his neck until he laughs. She's a walking advertisement for blissful motherhood. *What on earth is more important or precious than this?* I can almost hear her say for the ad campaign. She would look down at the babe with soft eyes, and he would reach up a chubby hand to pat her face. *Nothing* is the answer. Nothing is more important or precious on this earth.

"You could adopt," Shana says bluntly over lunch in the city. I nearly choke on my mouthful of mustard greens. It takes all my control not to backhand her across the face—with my left hand, the one with the wedding ring (still). She goes on pontificating about adoption, why she and Damon feel so lucky they didn't have to go that route, but what a viable, worthy route it is, one that would mark me as a saint for the rest of my days—especially as the single mother of an adopted child! What a hero I would be! She doesn't say *that* outright, of course, but she is so worked up by the end over my imaginary adoption of a needy child (or children!) that her eyes shine with tears. Meanwhile, I haven't said a word. She must think I'm overcome—with the idea of my imaginary family and my unending gratitude for the stalwart friend who has buoyed me through this dark time with her brilliant advice. She puts her hand over mine before we pay the bill. For a moment I think *she* might pay the bill, in her state of near euphoria, which I *would* be grateful for—but she doesn't.

When I get home, I wriggle my finger free of the ring at last. There's a white band of squeezed skin underneath that hasn't seen light or air in years. Instead of tossing the ring out the window, as part of me would like to do, I set it in the corner of my top dresser drawer, under my overwashed underpants.

*

I walk into class with a frown embedded in my body and soul. As soon as the door shuts behind me, though, I look up and smile. The friendly professor—it's an act that continues to save me. I set a chilled can of Diet Coke down on the desk, and Bernardo, one of my most outgoing students, points at it. "Those'll kill you, Professor," he says. "Before cigarettes?" I ask, lightning-quick. Everyone laughs: Joanne, Simon, Mary, Devon, James, the silent Chloe—and Bernardo, of course. He chuckles and shakes his head. The funny, friendly professor.

It has crossed my mind to fuck one of them. They're adult students, after all—some are divorced, or have casual girlfriends. It wouldn't take much. Pulling someone aside—Bernardo maybe, with his dark eyes and extravagant lashes. We've talked after class, bantered and flirted a bit. I could just say, "Want to get a drink?" one night. Go freshen my lipstick in the harsh fluorescent light of the school restroom. Have a few glasses of wine at a nearby bar. Touch his leg. Let him take me home and touch me all over.

But that would not be appropriate for someone in my position. For a *professor*. Though I'm hardly a professor. I'm a non-tenure-track lecturer at an overpriced, second-rate city school, teaching evening classes to returning students. The school seems to be struggling; I've heard rumors, and I can read the signs. My class, Survey of Western Verse II, 1850–Present, a standard in the literature program, was so small that the dean almost axed it at the start of the semester; I had another that *was* cancelled due to low enrollment. In the days just after Nathan left, when I veered from mania to despair and back again, I imagined using my extra time to take kickboxing classes at the local gym, transforming myself into a fighter, like the actress would do in one of her films. But I've gone nowhere near the gym, and I'm still the same person I was weeks ago. Aside from the financial blow, cushioned only by our still-joint savings account, all the class loss has done is make these days even emptier. I should have offered to teach anything—even Intro Composition to freshmen, which I swore I'd never teach again—if only to save myself from these long, blank days.

After class, I come back to my barely maintained, barely still elegant brownstone alone. I climb the stairs, nearly wheezing by the end. The wheezing is new—the consequence of reviving my grad school smoking habit after Nathan left. Though I've never thought, not even once, *I should quit smoking;* I've only thought, *I should move.* We always talked about moving *when the baby came.* Ha. If I were forced to move now, I'd have to leave the neighborhood—and in many ways, that would be a relief. To escape the entitled, ever-breeding bourgeoisie. I can't sit in a café here, grading or reading, for twenty minutes without some mom coming to buy her kids overpriced pastries while managing them in loudly hushed tones. It does more than grate on my nerves—it drives a spike into my side. Even worse is to look up and see a cherubic face close to mine, eyes blinking at me, curious and killing.

If someone could walk by my window (thankfully they can't; the most they can see from the street is the light from my lamps and the shadow of the slowly turning ceiling fan), they'd see a charmless place, full of Ikea furniture and shabbily stacked books. And a middle-aged woman, alone with a cat, glass of cheap wine in hand. A cliché, a "cat lady," a laughingstock.

I never pursued money. I thought it would come to me. I did! I thought the life of the mind would deliver it up in a matter of years—that my PhD in literature, with a specialization in poetry, of all things, would elevate me in ways that weren't merely intellectual. That, in addition to being feted and admired as a scholar of great renown, I would have job security. Health insurance. Steady, and steadily rising, income. "But who's going to hire you?" Nathan would tease, secure in his practical Doctorate of Education program. I didn't like to worry over such troublesome details. In grad school, Nathan and I would sit in the library with our heads bent over books, under the green glow of old-fashioned desk lamps. At a corner table, away from the rabble. As I read deeper into John Berryman's *The Dream Songs*, I felt my cheeks flush and my heart rate accelerate. When I couldn't contain my ecstatic fervor anymore—over the strange and glorious diction, the untamed turns of phrase—I shoved the book under Nathan's nose as if to say, *See? This is what matters. This.* At the time, Nathan raised his eyebrows as he scanned the page, and when he finished, he nodded. "Good stuff," he said, "very good," as if he were praising a child's efforts at drawing instead of the masterful set of poems I'd shared. Such passion for poetry I had back then! That was where "the life of the mind" took root: what a joke! I could roll on the floor in hysterics at such naïveté now, if it were at all funny. The life of the mind! *FUCK* the life of the mind.

*

In the morning, I head out for one of my long, slow walks. Ever since Nathan left, I've felt the urge to ramble—through our gentrified bubble, out to the edges where the natural foods stores and sparsely filled niche boutiques give way to cramped bodegas and dilapidated hardware stores. Past those, even, to the old warehouse district near the water, all the way down, once, to the waterfront park where enormous old cranes stand like sentinels over the few illegal fishermen on the pier. At first, going walking was just a way to not feel, after Nathan. Or a different way *to* feel—because I couldn't *not* feel, really, feelings bombarded me, ruled me, yanked me here and there like a sad marionette—but to feel while moving in a forward direction somehow helped, gave me some sense of control. Walking pushed the misery along through my body, distracting me from my grief the way a deep sleep can, though without the sharp pain of waking up. Returning home at the end of a walk was much less horrible—it hurt, but in a dull, dry, mostly bearable way, that at least made me feel anchored in something, in my tired and aching body instead of my pulverized heart.

I once stopped in a church—in the early, desperate days— and pushed into the dim, silent interior. Got awkwardly to my knees on one of the velvet-padded knee rests and bent my head, and prayed, or tried to pray. *What if the actress could see me now—what would she think?* I wondered, kneeling there. Would she study me, as if for a potential future role? Take note of the angle at which I inclined my head? Or the way I clasped my hands together, like a child? The way my body shook with sobs, and shook harder, perhaps, at the thought of her watching?

Or would she glance at me and simply shake her head? *Peasants*, she'd think. *Always throwing themselves on the mercy of the divine.*

Nothing happened in the church that day. No angels descended on a wave of iridescent light. No booming voice told me I'd recover, that everything would turn out fine. I struggled to my feet after a while, feeling, at least, wholly cried out for the time being.

Coming back from my walk a few hours later, I see a large cardboard box in front of the actress's house. It wasn't there when I left, but how long has it been sitting there? What did I miss? I breeze right past my own building and speed-walk to number 202. Like everyone else around here, like one of *the people*, the actress puts out her family's castoffs on a fairly regular basis—books they've finished, shoes and clothes they've outgrown, furniture they no longer want, etc.—for passersby to pick up. Our neighborhood is a kind of slow-trickle flea market. You can grab a board game from the steps of one house, then walk a block or two and find a cute handbag. Or a DVD collection. Or a Lego set. Nathan and I found this incredibly charming, not to mention useful, when we first moved here. The actress—or one of her *staff*, I'm sure—arranges her giveaways neatly in a box, or hangs them from the spikes of the fence, or lines them up below it, on the sidewalk itself. I've snagged every single thing of hers I've seen, sometimes coming home with armfuls of sweaters and kids' rain boots, or teetering up the stairs (once) with a heavy, ornate side table. I like to think I've gotten everything she's ever put out, but is that even possible? Surely I've missed things when I was at work, or out of town, or simply not paying enough attention. As I get closer to the box, my heart pounding in my chest, I wonder if anyone beat me to this particular haul. The box is still there, but is everything in place? I wish I could present the actress with an inventory list so I could know for certain that I have it all.

Then a neighbor turns out of her own gate, right in front of me, and blocks my view of the box. *She's heading straight for it.* I arrive just behind her, panting and sweating. "Hi," she says, but I'm staring down intently, cataloguing the contents. There's a pile of bound and published screenplays of 1990s films like *Glengarry Glen Ross* and *Sex, Lies, and Videotape*; a small rectangular mirror framed in mother-of-pearl; and a wooden elephant on wheels. This is a good haul. A *very* good haul. I finally look up at the neighbor. She's around my age, with a head of frizzy gray-brown hair and horn-rimmed glasses sliding down her nose. *There's nothing for you here, sister*, I want to snarl. *Move along.* I watch tensely as she bends down and picks up the top screenplay, the one for

Glengarry Glen Ross. As she flips the pages, I stand there saying, *Drop it. Drop it. Drop it.* In my head, over and over. Finally, she looks up, smiles awkwardly, and . . . just when I think she might try to walk off with the prize, just when I imagine ripping it from her hands . . . she tosses it carelessly back in the box—like it's trash!—and walks off. I want to lean against the actress's fence in relief, but there's no time. I pick up the whole box and carry it home, feeling happiness well up inside me for the first time in days.

At first, Nathan teased me lightheartedly about my fixation on the actress's discarded belongings, but by the end I was sure he meant his remarks to hit my tender spots. "Why do you want that thing?" he said once, frowning at a colorful rattle I'd collected. This was after failed IVF cycle number four. Or five. I'm not sure. They all blur together after a while. What he meant was, *Why do you want that stuff if you can't even have a baby?* I accused him of being cruel. He said he hadn't meant it that way, it was just that we didn't have the room to store extra things, but of course we did—we had the "baby's room."

That's not what we called it. We called it "the study" because there was a (mostly unused) desk in there. We called it "the guest room" because there was a twin bed in there, the one I'd dragged with me from one apartment to the next since grad school. We called it "the storage room" because there were two closets in there, crammed with family photo albums, old books, clothes, and a beach umbrella for our infrequent trips to the shore. But we never, ever, called it "the baby's room," though we both knew very well that's what it would be, should be, should have been. Of course, in my own head, I'd already renovated it—thrown out the old twin, finally, organized the closets and put unwanted items, the refuse of our younger years, out front, and moved the desk to a corner of the living room. Put up a playful border. Installed a crib with a mobile of black-and-white squares hanging over it. Added a dresser and changing table, and a child's small table and chairs. I'd even moved things around—in my head—throughout the years of our trying. Put the crib closer to the window, then away from it to lessen the noise from the street. Pulled down one border, a girly one, and put up another with trains and airplanes. Then I replaced that with a gender-neutral one patterned with triangles, circles, and squares in grays and blacks— like the mobile. I'd patted my round belly. Smoothed my hands over the firm dome of flesh. Sunk into the tacky calico-patterned glider and rocked myself to sleep.

Later, I saw one pair of worn, thong-style Birkenstocks out in front of their house. A woman's size 8, I'd guess. Probably *hers*. Got 'em.

*

Tonight the long-lashed, dark-eyed Bernardo looked at my left hand and asked, "What happened to your wedding band?" They're like that, my students, bluntly curious about my life. Mary, an older woman with cropped gray hair, shook her head and tsked at him. I flashed my best game-face smile and said, "Don't worry, Bernardo, I'm just having it cleaned." He nodded like he believed me but Mary gave me a look. My performance must have faltered somewhere. Was there a false note in my voice? Was my smile too big? I had to remember to wear my damn ring next time. And make sure it looked extra-shiny.

We used to sleep spooned together all night long. If Nathan flipped over, I would flip, too. We were always touching: my belly pressed against his back, his back rooted to my belly.

The actress's house is dark tonight. Maybe they've gone upstate for the weekend. They'll stop at a farm stand on the way to buy fresh corn and tomatoes, melons and blueberries. The farmer will say, "I know your face!" in his rustically charming manner—so much better than the hard stares she gets in the city. She'll smile under the brim of her hat and bounce the baby gently on her hip as I've seen her do. Her husband will usher them all back to the safety of the car. They'll drive down a wooded lane. Step into a tastefully furnished getaway cabin. Deep peace in the shade of trees. Sweet familial harmony. Anonymity at last! The actress will cast off her hat and laugh. *Cut.*

If it were a certain kind of nineties movie, though, things would go horribly wrong. Some leering man would come to the door one evening asking politely for help with his car but sending chills up the actress's spine. They would refuse him, and then, in the dead of night, he'd come back and start a campaign of subtle terror against them. The children would huddle in a closet. The ineffectual city dad would stand by the door, sweat beading his forehead, fireplace poker in hand. And the actress, wide-eyed, would look out at the darkness through a crack in the curtains; she'd scream when the man's pale face popped into view, right up against hers but for the thin layer of glass.

But no, the actress is still around—I run into her on the street the next morning. "Running into her" makes it sound as if we're old friends who would stand on the sidewalk for a moment, trading updates on our personal lives. As if I'd remark on how beautifully the baby is gaining weight—*You're breastfeeding him?* (*Of course, of course.*) As if she would lay a cool, dry hand on my arm and ask how I'd been doing, in a knowing voice. As if her knowing about the terrible breakup could make the clenched sadness in me dissipate, at least for a little while. As if I'd feel comfortable enough to tear up a little, right there on the sidewalk, with the actress's hand on my arm.

Nothing like that happens, of course. I don't "run into her": I'm leaving the house, just opening my gate, when she whisks by wearing black cropped pants with high heels and a flowing blue silk top. *Water*, I think, watching her move. Is she on her way to a hair appointment? A meeting in the city? A consultation about a script? I'm just leaving to go to the grocery store in the worn brown-and-red-striped cotton dress I think of as my summer uniform. In forty minutes or so I'll return, lugging bags full of "single woman" food: one bunch of broccoli, instant couscous, red beans, basmati rice, boxes of frozen lasagna and palak paneer, and one small bag of Doritos, my "treat." When the actress passed by, she didn't turn or nod or make any gesture to show that she'd noticed me. But I *know* she did. I stand and watch her all the way up the block.

She was wearing our lipstick today, as usual. I say "our" because, while I doubt her lipstick is L'Oréal's #762 Divine Wine, it *is* a velvety reddish-brown matte like mine. And she seems to wear it all the time, like I do—whether she's running an errand or going out for the night. I wear mine everywhere, too—I put it on and watch it bring my face to life. Nathan used to laugh at me whenever I said I looked *like death* without my lipstick—but it's true. It's always been true, even when I was younger. He might agree with me now, if he could see the haggard woman who greets me in the mirror every morning. *Go ahead and paint your lips, honey,* he'd say, sucking down one of his kale smoothies.

Later that same night, I pause by her house on my way home from work. Lights on in the kitchen. The actress stands at the island, opening a bottle of wine. Children in bed. The husband upstairs somewhere. Alone with a bottle of wine, how luxurious. I'll be alone with one, too, in a few minutes, but the quality of her aloneness differs from mine. Hers is fuller: surrounded, swaddled even—an island on whose shores laps a vibrant, busy sea. Her aloneness is temporary; mine is infinite. Mine spreads out from the center like a puddle, muddying everything it touches. Even the cat shrinks back, slinks to dry land. But there the actress is on her cozy island, pouring a generous glass of good white wine that's been chilled just for her by some thoughtful staff member who then slipped away to leave her in peace. She takes her first sip while standing there, and then sips again, quickly, like it's too delicious to wait. When have I tasted wine like that?

In the early days of our relationship, Nathan and I went to Napa for a long weekend. I was presenting a paper at the MLA conference in San Francisco, so we rented a car one day and drove through the rolling golden-brown hills, stopping at every vineyard whose name we even remotely recognized. We were drunk within an hour. There was one wine, a red, maybe a Pinot Noir? We loved it. We bought a whole case and dealt with the hassle of shipping it home. But once we were back, sitting at the table in my sparsely furnished studio, trying the first sip from the first of the bottles, it tasted all wrong: vinegary, acidic. Cheap, though it wasn't. Not at all like it had tasted out there—full of warmth—a glass of deep, mellow, earthy richness.

I bite into a Red Delicious apple—Nathan's favorite. It's mealy, as they always are. Tastes gray. I have no idea what he sees in them, or why I bought six of these at the grocery store. They were right next to the crisp and tasty Fujis, but I couldn't help grabbing them. Knowing I would hate them. Knowing I would take a single bite and throw them one after the other into the trash.

*

Early in her career, the actress was praised for tackling complicated roles. Damaged women—women who'd been

LAURA SIMS

abused or raped but who went on fighting valiantly through life. Tough, unlikable women, women with attitude and chutzpah and strong moral beliefs. Women who could stand up to a school board or a corporate tycoon but who, privately, were addicts or bad mothers or engaged in minor fraud. You love them, but you also want to keep them at arm's length. Is that who I am? Do I deserve to be loved, or even liked? Nathan has said no. And now I hear the world repeat it after him: *no, no, no, no, no.* Every day since he left. It echoes through the streets and against the walls of the buildings and comes back to me, smacking me squarely in the face: NO.

My body, also, has firmly said no. *You are not worthy of carrying life. You are not one of those women, the ones entrusted with sacred purpose.* Or is it *encrusted*? Am I not worthy, even, of being encrusted with sacred purpose, with the life that clings and ages and erodes a woman from the moment it forms?

So what made the actress turn from those roles, those admirable lives in the gray area, to those that exist only in black and white? Or electric blue, like the costume she wears in the new blockbuster. What made her choose to become fodder for bus-side posters? Money, I'd guess. Ambition. Middle age (or close enough). Those kids. All those kids— they have to be fed.

Does she dream at night of their gaping, hungry mouths? Of falling, disappearing, into the void of motherhood? Not that *she* could ever disappear—but she might fear it anyway. Tonight in class we discussed a haiku by Buson— one of the ways I like to diverge from the strictures of the Western Verse curriculum. "The camellia – / it fell into the darkness / of the old well." I tried to make my students see the beauty and horror of the poem—the bright white swallowed by limitless darkness, the white lighting the dark as it sinks down, down—but Simon and Bernardo in particular refused to take it at anything more than surface value. I thought of the actress falling, mouth agape, hands waving in air, white linen sundress billowing in the updraft, into nothingness. Consumed. It gave me a moment's plea- sure—and a thrill of fear. *Don't!* I would scream, reaching my arms down the well. But then I would linger, waiting for the distant splash. "It's pretty," Bernardo said, shrugging. "Don't try to make it so complicated, Professor." He sat there, grinning impishly. "It's horrific," I snapped. I saw him pull back into himself a tiny bit, and felt satisfied. "Think of her—the camellia—sinking down in full flower, lost forever to darkness. It's a horror story." Joanne, Mary, and Chloe nodded in response: they could see it. Simon had lost interest, was consulting his phone. Bernardo still looked puzzled. Not the brightest spark, Bernardo, but definitely the hottest.

"You made up with your husband," Bernardo had said almost as soon as I walked in the door. I had the newly polished wedding ring back in place. He grinned slyly. Flustered, I folded my arms over my chest and started class as breezily as I could. I'd dug the ring out of my dresser drawer and taken it to a jewelry store for buffing. I promised myself I'd throw it into the river as soon as the semester ended. Bernardo's grin stayed fixed, like he wouldn't let go of the "joke"—or of me. Bright white teeth. The bastard.

I stared into the hall bathroom mirror after class and said "I am unloved" out loud. I hated watching my dry lips move. Do my students hate watching them move as much as I do? By the end of class, even though I'd just been standing there talking, I'd become a wan and sickly old woman. But I knew how to fix that—I scrounged in my purse for Divine Wine and applied it liberally. Blotted it, applied again. Topped it with Burt's Bees for a touch of shine. *Great* improvement. It even lifted my spirits somewhat. Because it made me think of the actress? Perhaps. At least, a little bit.

*

I'm in a second-run theater with cramped seats watching a recent film of the actress's—not the one from the bus poster, but the one that came out just before it, a subpar

thriller. I've already seen it. She plays a detective whole-
heartedly committed to her job—because the rest of her
life is a mess. Or else I have it mixed up: *as a result* of her
commitment to her job, the rest of her life is a mess. It's
hard to say which. I note the details of what I suppose could
be called the detective's "home life": the empty fridge, the
amply filled liquor cabinet, the permanently unmade bed,
the nightly insomnia, and, of course, the latest broken
romance. *You're playing me and you don't even know it.* I pick up
my bag of popcorn and tilt the remains into my mouth.

In the end, she catches the serial killer and finds a promising new love interest. Lucky her. Now she gets to go
home to her immaculate, well-appointed brownstone and
be a beloved mother, a gifted wife, and a rich, famous person. And me? I get to go home to one floor of an empty,
neglected brownstone. And to Cat.

I sit there for a long time in the half-light of the theater,
watching the credits roll. I want to delay that moment
when I walk through the lobby doors, smack into the wall
of oppressive heat and sunlight. Crowded sidewalks and
blaring horns. Can't I just stay here? And merge with the
dark? Nathan used to sit with me as the credits rolled—he
would never rush me out as people stood, gathered their
coats and bags, and hustled down the aisle. He understood.

Why should we rush back out there, to the complexities and letdowns of real life? It was one of the things I loved about him—his ability to savor the post-movie darkness with me. To sit as though the two of us were safe in a cave where no one and nothing could reach us.

I think life must have been easier for early humans, crouching and sheltering in caves. When the only form of entertainment was watching shadows move on the rock walls, in the firelight. When what mattered was shielding our tribe from saber-toothed tigers. Giant bears. There were *actual* dangers then—not beautiful, loose-limbed women gliding across the screen and past our doors in costly dresses and costly versions of our own drugstore lipstick, showing us who we aren't, what we haven't done, can't do, and will never have.

Of course, in ancient times I would have been exiled for my barrenness. Out of the cave, woman, away from the fire. Into the snow with a spear (perhaps) and a bearskin coat, to wander the rocky terrain. Until I was eaten or fatally injured or froze to death. I admire the cleanness and honesty of such an expulsion; I would have been able to taste and touch an emptiness like that.

Coming home, I turn onto my block and nearly collide with the actress's husband. He's jogging, but he holds his hands out and stops, says, "Sorry," at the same time I do. We lock eyes for a moment. I can tell he's evaluating me. I can tell he likes what he sees. He smiles, gives a nod, and takes off running up the street. On his way to the park, no doubt. At nearly 10 p.m.? I suppose he can do what he likes. The kids are in bed and the actress is having her wine. But why doesn't he join her? Isn't that what married couples with kids do at the end of the day? Relax and reconnect? Watch a show? Perhaps they've had a fight and he's sweating it out. When he comes back, the air will have cleared. She'll pour him a glass of icy water, bottled and brought direct to them by special shipment from the streams of the Swiss Alps. He'll wrap his hand around hers when he takes the glass, and the tension will evaporate. Whatever. All that matters is that the husband and I had a moment. I rarely give him a thought, but . . . he has gorgeous dark eyes. And strong, shapely legs. I like his hair how it is now, nearly down to his shoulders, though it was tied back for the jog. I've never been with a man with such long hair. Or with such a full beard. The feeling of our moment tingles at the ends of my fingers and toes.

*

The next day at lunch, Shana says, "You seem better." When I roll my eyes she says, "Really! You do! I'm not just saying that!" Shana has the social savvy of a wild boar. I lift my wineglass and feel color rush to my cheeks. The aftereffects of my moment with the husband still linger, even into this new day. "Are you seeing someone?" she asks, tilting her head. I stare down into my wine and smile. Shake my head so my hair falls charmingly into my face. She taps my hand triumphantly. "You *are!*" she says, raising her voice. I shush her and she whisper-shouts, "You're *seeing* someone!" I almost correct her and say, *No, it's nothing,* but then I don't. What do I care what Shana thinks? If I tell her I'm seeing someone, she'll leave me alone, stop checking in via phone and text with her caring condescension. "I might be," I say coyly. Shana looks straight at me then and says, "What a relief. Honestly, that's a big relief." That stops me cold. Why have I maintained this friendship, built on the bonding that took place over a shitty admin job more than a decade ago? Shana and I are strangers, really—she knows nothing about me and has nothing I want. Nothing I need. I smile coldly and take a gulp of wine as she patters on. She doesn't even ask who it is, my new love interest, because she doesn't *really* care; she just wants to slough me off of her to-do list, so she can move on to discuss more interesting and rewarding topics pertaining to herself and her tidy little married life. The purchase of a new flat-screen TV for their living room. Her son's second-grade accomplishments, and her relief at having her daughter in preschool full-time, at last.

I manage to feign interest, concern, delight, even, at all the appropriate moments, but as we hug goodbye I'm saying, *Goodbye, goodbye, goodbye,* in my head, meaning it forever.

Cat greets me at the door with the same enthusiasm she used to show Nathan when he came home—pathetic creature. *Don't you know,* I want to say, *he's dumped you right along with me?* It's shocking that he has, actually, given their long history together. When we were trying to get pregnant he'd drive me crazy by cuddling Cat to his chest and saying things like, "You'll always be my first baby," in a ridiculous little voice.

I have no use for the cat, though I go on keeping it alive. I whisper things into her delicate pink ear I would never say to a human, cruel things about loss and the death of love. The cat twitches her tail, flicks her ear like she's shooing a fly. Stalks away. But for the last few days, I've been good. Kind and attentive. Forgiving of Nathan's late ownership. Able to see how absurd it is to make an animal pay for its former master's sins. When I sit at my desk and the cat comes trotting to rub a figure eight around my legs, I pick her up and put her on my lap. I scratch under her chin like Nathan used to do, where the fur is soft and white. She purrs. So hard and loud it's disturbing. She's too desperate for love. I push her from my lap and flick the hair she's left behind off my jeans.

The next time I see the actress's husband, he'll veer toward me on the street. Brush the right side of my body, stoking a quick wave of heat. Then he'll stop, gesturing in the direction of his house. In the direction of *her* house. *No one's home,* he'll say. *Want to come over?* He'll grab my hand and guide me through their front garden, down to the basement entrance, the family's most intimate door. I'll duck my head when I enter and step over the entryway, as I've seen visitors to temples and shrines do. He'll turn to face me, pull me toward that glorious kitchen island of theirs. His warm hands will be on my hips, but I'll be staring all around—at the floor where she walks, at the ceiling that hangs over her, at the paintings and family photos on the walls and the pots and pans I've seen gleaming through the window. The husband won't seem to notice, or mind. Before I know it, my bare ass will be up on the island and he'll be pushing his dick deep inside me. Now cue the grunting and groaning as we really start to move, cue the pots and pans shaking above us on their hooks. My hands are in his hair but I keep my eyes glued to a black-and-white photo of the five of them, tumbled up together on a green lawn, all sunglasses and grins. When the husband comes, when he collapses against me and breathes hot air onto my neck, the picture drops from the wall. The glass shatters.

*

I feel like a star tonight, standing before my class of over-worked adult students. Their collective gaze warms me—it fills my belly with something like pleasure, mirth, belonging. I raise my voice and gesture emphatically as I explain Emily Dickinson's biography—her historically exaggerated reclu-siveness, her correspondence with the great thinkers of the day, her outsized, seemingly erotic passion for God. They're all hooked, every one. *I love you, my dears.* Chloe shifts in her seat and smiles as though she has heard me.

But Bernardo seems to be sulking tonight. He frowns during lecture, averts his eyes when I look at him. He is not at all his usual perky, impertinent self. I find myself directing questions and comments to him, prodding him to speak. He gives only the most perfunctory responses. It doesn't stop me from being my most effusive and alive, though. Bernardo's resistance is nothing more than a minor itch. I'm on an Emily Dickinson high, and I feel like cramming her sharp little words and lines down their throats. I mean, lovingly. Adoringly, even. It would be so good for them, so nourishing. I recite the first stanza of poem number 249: "Wild Nights – Wild Nights! / Were I with thee / Wild Nights should be / Our luxury!" while remembering how the actress's husband's face contorted when he came. Does he make the same face with *her?* I wonder. Joanne, a fortysomething singleton like me, looks down at the page with a dour face. "What was she doing, alone in her room, writing this weird stuff?" she asks. "Oh, Joanne," I say. The class laughs. Joanne reddens, but smiles. I think of my legs veed up in the air on the actress's island, of the actress's husband pounding away, right on the spot where she has her nightly glass of wine! What glory! *Wild Nights!*

After class, Bernardo stays stuck to his seat. Finally, when the last student has left and we're alone, he clears his throat but says nothing. "What's up?" I ask lightly. I'm floating on air. It's hard for me to focus on his face with filthy images of the actress's husband crowding my mind. Finally, Bernardo speaks: "Professor, I don't get why you gave me a C." It's his paper, of course. He waves it around, and then slaps it down on his desk. "Oh," I say warmly. "Come up here and I'll walk you through it." I see something flicker in his eyes, some tension releasing. I'll have him grinning again soon.

Next time, the husband and I will meet in the park, late at night, when he goes for one of his runs. We'll clasp hands and walk the main loop until we reach the head of a narrow, winding trail leading into the woods. We'll follow it over one small hill and down to a gazebo in a secluded clearing. The scene will be almost unbearably picturesque in the moonlight. Pausing to take it in, we'll look at each other's strange faces, and after some time he'll lead me into the gazebo, lay me down on the narrow bench where homeless people sleep and shoot up and rats crawl and babies' dirty diapers are changed by harried mothers, and he'll fuck me long and hard and his smooth dark beard will brush against my face while his heart beats in time with mine.

Imagine the actress discovering us! On our crusty gazebo bench. On the kitchen island, my legs raised in a V. Her lip would curl at the sight of me. *Her?* she'd ask, incredulous. *She's just one of the neighbors, for Christ's sake.* But wouldn't it make us sisters of a kind, the actress and me? Wouldn't it be an act of communion with her, in the end? Could I ever make her see it that way?

Bernardo's eyes have cleared, but he looks puzzled. What was I saying? Right. "So if you want to revise, I'll give you a whole new grade." He smiles. "Clean slate?" he asks. "Clean slate," I agree.

*

The next morning, I stare into the small green plot shielding, but not obscuring, the garden-level windows to the actress's house: ferns, a small, leafy tree, window boxes hanging from the gate. All dense and artfully overgrown.

But not wild. Not wild. Calm down. I close my eyes for a moment. I can see the gazebo, pale and glittering under the moon, but that's all. The gazebo is empty. The kitchen is empty, the kitchen island bare. I've been locked out of the scene.

When I go back inside, my phone's ring is screaming through the apartment. Cat sits by the window, cleaning her paws. On the screen it says: *Nathan.* Those letters, arranged in that order, raise a wall of black before my eyes. I back away from the phone. Eventually the screeching ends.

Time passes. I don't know how much time. I'm sitting on the couch, where I've been since . . . the call. In the early days, after the breakup, I longed to see his name on my phone screen, to hear his voice in my ear, to hear him saying, *I fucked up, I'll come back, please, please forgive me.* The call that never came. Cat winds herself around my legs, mewing plaintively for dinner. When I look up at the window, I see the light has shifted. The angle and quality of the light. Without warning, we're lodged inside the sad husk of late afternoon and I'm spooning food into Cat's dirty bowl.

I pour myself a large glass of wine. I will not give in to fear. I put the message on speaker—somehow I can handle it better that way. Or I think I can. His smooth, deep, deeply familiar voice fills the room. My skin literally crawls. I scratch my neck and then the backs of my hands as he speaks.

"Hey. Hi. Uh—this is, this is awkward. But I—I really want to pick up Cat sometime, and her stuff. Is there a good day I could do that? I still have keys, so I could—you know, you don't have to be there. Let me know. Hope you're well."

You'd expect me to pick up the phone and throw it. Or scream. I don't. I feel perfectly fine. That damn cat. He doesn't care about her—he never did! That's why she has no name but Cat! For fuck's sake. He loves her as much as I do, which is: a negligible amount. Infinitesimal. Ludicrous— he wants to take Cat back, the final vestige of our life together. Ha!

I guzzle half the glass of wine. Time for a walk.

Dickinson's poems are full of sex and rage, I told my students the other night. I quoted the lines "Come slowly – Eden! / Lips unused to Thee – / Bashful – sip thy Jessamines – / As the fainting bee." I said, "She wanted God to come to her, she feared he would come to her—and he did. She got what she wanted, in the end." *I got nothing,* I think as I wander, skating my eyes over worn faces hungry faces scared faces glowing happy faces, all evening long.

It's the wine or it's the fast slippage of time that pulls me along for hours before I realize my fatigue. My aching feet. I return to my block at last and stand outside the actress's house. It is 9 p.m. I see her husband in there, phone to his ear, showing his white teeth, insatiable wolf.

If he were to come out tonight he would see me sweaty and disheveled, with wine breath and wild hair. He would like me like that: flawed and mussed, so unlike his wife. But the wolf won't come out. There will be no island, no gazebo, no dark beard in the moonlight. The wolf is really a dog, a good dog lying at its mistress's feet, obedient and true.

Still, I can't seem to move from my post in front of their house. Inside my apartment is the phone and inside the phone is *Nathan*. His voice. His demands. As always, his demands—even after he's gone he makes demands, but this one I refuse to meet. He will not take Cat! I won't give her up. Something like love wells up inside me, surprising me with its force—love for poor Cat, rejected and broken like me. I feel shaken and have to bend over, hands on my knees, breathing deeply by the actress's gate.

I'm still trembling there when I hear a door open. Someone's coming out of the house. It's too late for me to move so I stay put, hoping I'm invisible in the night. Footsteps. I can't see anything but I *know* it's him. He stops at the gate, clears his throat. "You all right?" He sounds wary. I straighten up and look into his handsome, frowning face. I want to see welcome there—or recognition, or lust—but his face is blank. The mask someone wears when he's looking at a weird stranger standing too close to his family home. "I'm fine," I say, mumbling, and speed-walk up the street, away from the actress's husband.

*

I wake the next morning to the sight of Cat stretched out beside me on the bed, bathing her chest with her tongue. She's happy here. This is her *home*. Nathan can't have her. If he'd wanted to keep her, he should have taken her when he left.

I'm steering clear of the actress's house for a while. I cross the street to the opposite side. I circle the whole block to avoid walking by. It's like pushing Reset, like Bernardo rewriting his paper for a whole new grade.

The block party looms. By then, Nathan will have lost interest in Cat. I'll celebrate my freedom, and Cat's, with my dear neighbors. I'll wear a brightly colored strapless dress and high-heeled sandals like hers. I'll buy food from the gourmet store where the actress shops and arrive breathless, carrying artfully stamped and packed paper bags. I'll get pleasantly tipsy without descending into sloppy drunkenness. I'll flirt with the men my age and younger—single or married. I'll wear "our" shade of lipstick. Someone might even mistake me for her, at first, one of the old-timers on the block. They'll say, "Sorry—I thought you were *her*," and I'll blush attractively, touch my hair and say, "Honest mistake." I'll spare an affectionate glance for the kids in the bouncy house, jumping for joy. *I know that feeling!* I'll want to shout. *I'm jumping on the inside, just like you!* And then that old bag, Mrs. H, will sidle up and ask with a sneer in her voice, "Which one is yours?"

*

I said yes to lunch with Shana only because I didn't have the energy to explain that I never wanted to see her again. I sit here telling her all the right things in between sips of iced tea. I requested we meet at a sleek lunch spot in the city. I'm wearing one of my most flattering dresses, the dark red one with a deep V-neck and a tightly cinched waist. I'm even wearing heels. I've gathered my hair into a sophisticated bun, and worn the dangly gold earrings that accentuate the long curve of my neck. I warm to the appreciative looks I'm getting from our waiter and every other man in the room.

Shana doesn't seem to notice everyone noticing me. She's squinting at me like there's something wrong, but I go on as if I haven't noticed. "Oh my god, guess what? Nathan is trying to get Cat! He wants to take Cat from me. Can you believe it?" I lean close to her over the table, lowering my voice, nearly whispering through my perfectly matte red lips as if I were starring in the actress's lone spy movie, the one where she is a double agent who convinces everyone around her, everyone who comes in contact with her, that she's on *their* side. Shana fools with her glass, turns it by the stem. Won't meet my eyes. "You don't like the cat, though. Right? And wasn't it his? I mean originally?"

The waitress—I'd thought we had a waiter, but somehow I was wrong—comes to take our plates. In the silence I refuse to fill, I look at the tables around us. All the men in the room have vanished. All I see are women like us, middle-aged, carefully coiffed and dressed, hunching over their salads in twos and threes. Picking at leaves of spinach. Goat cheese. Walnuts. Beets. Sipping iced tea or chilled white wine. Talking animatedly. The talk like a stream, like an unending buzz. I can hear my heart inside of the noise, pounding against it. *No. No, Shana. You are not right.*

I don't say a word, but signal for the check. I watch Shana, flustered, collect her expensive-but-dowdy cardigan off the back of her chair and rummage through her designer-knockoff purse for her wallet. I'm fairly certain she can feel the waves of hatred and disgust coming off of me. *I hate you. And I hate this place, full of clucking hens like us. I won't do this again. I mean it this time.*

Nathan has called and left another message. Less tentative this time. More insistent. "I'll come by Saturday morning to pick her up. Pack up her stuff. I'll call or text when I'm there." Mr. In Charge. Mr. Taking Control. Ha! That's what he thinks.

*

There she is, the actress. Stepping out, with the baby in his carrier, looking fresh, fit, well rested, and happy. Not carefully toned and preserved, like the lunching ladies, but effortlessly beautiful—like a handful of ripe berries just before you pop them into your mouth. After having not seen her, after having avoided her house for a brief little while because of what happened with the husband, the sight of her makes me squint. How does one get to live such a charmed life? How does one get to literally *have it all*? It strikes me as *funny*—that *billions* of us should be schlepping along, some of us barely surviving, while *one person* gets to be praised and lifted up by eternal light. When she passes my stoop without turning to look, I'm there with my cigarette in one hand, the other hand covering my mouth, convulsing with laughter.

The last time I laughed, really laughed, was with Nathan, watching that ridiculous buddy comedy about two cops who go undercover at a high school. One is fat and funny—the other is tall, handsome, and dumb. I'd been so reluctant to go—I knew it would be full of lighthearted woman-hating, and it was—but the physical stuff got me over and over again. The fat one falls in a pool. The fat one chugs beer and then barfs it back up. How I love to laugh! That deep-belly guffaw that's happening right now, that tells me: *I am not her! I never will be!* I may as well be the funny fat one myself. Why not? Stuff my face until I'm roly-poly, until I could roll right through the world and make people weep with laughter.

Mrs. H catches my eye when I pass her later on the way to the subway. "Haven't seen your husband around," she says matter-of-factly. Like she's pleased with herself and sorry for me all at once. Toxic combination. I don't need your pity, old thing! "No," I say, smiling sweetly, "you haven't."

I am sick to death of women. Kind women, careful women, strong-and-silent women, caretaking women, lonely women, old women, young women, perfect women, dead women, crazy women, haunted women, bitter women, hateful women, harsh women, hounded women, all women! I am not one of you! Leave me alone, leave me to the straight-forwardly horrible men.

*

Cat purrs contentedly in the morning sun. I look at her and feel soft and warm deep inside. Is this how mothers feel about their children? Nathan will never take you, darling one.

Like the fat one in the movie, I take pleasure in my farts these days. In the old days, I'd let one slip while we were sitting on the couch and laugh, but Nathan was always such a prude. He'd curl his upper lip and say, "Try to be a woman, why don't you?" It pleased and embarrassed me to make him sit in my stink—but it pleases me more now to sit on the cushions and let one rip with no consequences. The cat twitches her ears—that's all.

*

Early on Saturday morning the locksmith comes. When he's finished changing the locks I head out for a long day in the city. I'll tour the art galleries, have lunch at a charming bistro, see a matinee, and maybe even have dinner out, too, to be safe. I leave my phone at home, "by accident."

The day doesn't go quite as planned. I end up browsing in the city's last remaining large independent bookstore for a full two hours and leave with an armful of books and a searing headache. I'm dying of thirst. I step into the first bar I see, a slick-looking touristy place on the square. The wine is all right—I inhale the first glass and ask for another. Listen to the Minnesotans beside me debating the merits of the Giants versus the Jets. They may as well be at home on their sofas, nursing beers. Why bother coming to the city at all? Just so they can say they've been, I suppose. Maybe they hate it the whole time—the crowds, the noise, and the city dwellers' superior attitudes—and will feel a wave of relief on landing back at home. I stay at the bar until the 3 p.m. showing of *Dangerous Game*, that same thriller of the actress's I've seen before, still showing at the second-run theater a few blocks away.

The actress has been a prostitute, a private eye, a professor, a surgeon, a soldier, and a veterinarian with a soft spot for rodents. In today's film she is two things at once: a police officer posing as a prostitute. Hence the unsubtle title. The movie is just barely entertaining—especially on third viewing—moving quickly through all the tropes and twists you'd expect, so my mind is free to wonder: What will the actress's children think one day of her on-screen personae? If it were me, I'd feel a mingling of pride and disgust. Pride at her fame and wealth, disgust for a career made of putting on the lives of others. *You don't even know who you are, Mom! How can you tell me to be "myself"?* I can hear her daughter say one day soon, burning with adolescent resentment. But what's it to me? I've got my popcorn and a seat in the cozy dark, and today I have the pleasure of confounding Nathan, the quintessential bad guy of my life. My own movie would be titled, *Cat's Cradle*, and it, too, would be a blockbuster.

My phone is bright with texts when I get home. I glance at the screen and see that Nathan has filled it with all caps, like a screaming ransom letter. I leave it for morning, still wrapped in the imaginary haze of the movie's world, still buzzed from my successful day—and possibly the wine. Cat greets me effusively, sweet thing.

*

WHAT THE FUCK ARE YOU THINKING? CHANGING THE LOCKS?? HAVE YOU GONE

TOTALLY INSANE? YOU WERE ALREADY HALF-WAY THERE, NOW YOU'VE PLUNGED OVER THE EDGE. I WILL GET CAT BACK, BELIEVE ME.

Ha! That seals it. I would never hand Cat over to such a hateful, vindictive person, not in a million years. He would have to break the door down to get her—and Nathan is *not* a breaking-down-the-door kind of guy. He's a spineless shit, and his meaningless text-screaming proves it.

*

One thing that nags at me every time I pass the actress's house these days: a bright pink child's bike left leaning against the front of their house. In any other garden, this would have been stolen weeks ago. I once left a wooden chair in our front garden after refinishing it, so it could dry—I even hid it by the basement gate, out of sight from most angles. It was stolen overnight. One night! A measly chair! And the actress has the gall, the temerity, the rotten good *luck*, to leave this shiny, expensive little bike parked in full view for days on end with *no consequences*. She keeps it there, it seems, to show us how impenetrable her protective shield is, and to remind us how unprotected, how unspecial the rest of us are.

My fingers twitch when I pass the house. I have to fight myself to keep from grabbing the bike out in the open, in the middle of the day.

*

It's 2 a.m. I'm stepping through their front gate. Windows dark. Quiet. No alarm sounds, no net drops over me. I stride quickly to the bike, grab a handlebar in one hand and the seat in the other and lift it. It's light—like it's made of cardboard instead of metal. I run back on tiptoes, the bike held aloft, imagining how this would look from the outside: absolutely ludicrous. A middle-aged woman in all black, stealing a child's hot-pink bike at 2 a.m.! If it were a movie, I'd scoff. *Who writes this crap?* I'd say. When I reach my front door, I bend over, breathless. Beginning to laugh. I did it! Part triumph, part absurdity. But the end result: it's mine.

I store it in the extra room, where it looks ridiculous—and by that I mean: ridiculously *beautiful.* I leave the door cracked so I can glimpse it now and then. Cat saunters in, sniffs the front tire, and rubs her side against it. "Cat, come here," I say sharply. She looks at me—her gray eyes wide—and slumps down against the bike tire. Flicking her tail.

The next morning I turn my head ever so slightly as I pass the actress's house. Nothing has changed—I mean, nothing I haven't changed myself. I feel a thrill at the sight of their empty garden. Only leaves and plants now, separating them from us.

Nathan again, via text, of course. Not screaming this time. *Do I have to get a lawyer after you to get Cat back? She's my cat—she's always been my cat. You barely tolerated her. Be reasonable. Think of your allergies. Why would you want to hold on to Cat? I don't understand it. Please. Let's settle this like friends.*

Like friends! I won't write back—let him stew—but if I were going to, I'd write: *My allergies have magically disappeared. Thanks for your concern!*

*

The actress's middle child, the six-year-old, is riding a brand-new bike down the sidewalk. She'll soon pass right by my stoop. The bike is bright green, so shiny that it hurts my eyes. I can hardly see the girl's face under the giant helmet they have her wearing. As usual, the nanny saunters behind, smiling her contented smile. When you take a thing from someone like the actress, she merely replaces it. Before you know it, this new bike will be leaning against the front wall, too, as if nothing untoward ever happened, as if nothing untoward could ever happen again. If I were to take *this* bike, to try to prove them wrong, the next day a new one would stand in its place. And if I were to take *that* one, and so on . . . to infinity. I envision all the bright bikes piling up in my extra room, beginning to spill through the doorway into the living room—eventually I'd have to move to accommodate the endless bounty of the actress's life. I feel a tightness in my chest. I'm out in fresh air, under a cloudless blue sky, but suddenly I find it hard to breathe.

I go inside and masturbate. Angrily. On the worn couch, Cat curled on the floor beside me, undisturbed. When I'm spent, I find my breath again. It comes in gasps.

*

Tonight's class on Walt Whitman goes poorly. My head feels fuzzy. Like there's cotton wrapping my brain—squeezing it, even. Maybe it's Whitman, telling me "every atom belonging to me as good belongs to you." *Really?* I want to ask. *Is there really such balance in the universe?* I fumble for words, come out with the wrong ones. Mary stares at me in a sympathetic way, like she's saying, *Don't worry, the mind goes first as you age.* Bernardo keeps licking his lips. Is he high? Or just hot and dry in this stifling room? I tug at my neckline. The students are listless and underprepared. I let them go early, and after they've left I wander out to the city street.

At the bar a salesman type with his sleeves rolled up and his collar opened at the neck tries to convince me to fuck him. I'm quaking inside at the thought of *fucking someone other than Nathan*, but I act the part of the jaded city girl anyway. I tell him I'd do it right there, in the bathroom, if it were clean enough. But it's not—I know the bar well. I tell him I won't go anywhere else with him, that's it, that's our only non-option, and then I leave him sitting open-mouthed, somewhere between a laugh and a scowl, with his half-finished drink in his hand.

*

When I leave the house the next morning I see a used condom in the middle of the sidewalk, right in front of my house. As if what I teased the salesman with happened right here, a woman grasping the rails of my gate while getting taken from behind. When they were done, he just peeled off the rubber and dropped it. Right there, where people walk their dogs and children walk to school and women click by in heels on their way to jobs in needlelike office towers. I feel like someone has left me a soiled prize.

Silence from Nathan. Good. I don't want to hear his stupid voice, not even via text. I don't want to hear him wheedling or demanding ever again. I knew he'd let it go, leave the cat to me like a consolation prize. It shows what a cold and heartless prick he is, after all. Leave the useless cat to the barren woman and walk away into your bright new life.

Except: here he is. Nathan. On my stoop. Sitting there placidly, coffee from our favorite neighborhood café in hand. Our usual barista probably served him, gave him a fist bump and asked, *Where you been, man? How's things?* Meanwhile, the guy never even seems to recognize me. People have always preferred friendly, chatty Nathan to . . . whatever it is I seem to be. Uptight? Reserved? Unfriendly, even? And now here he sits, on the stoop, looking like he owns the place—which we never did, never could have, not in a million years. Even so, he sits there like a fucking king. The condom from earlier has disappeared—probably tidied up by Mrs. H—and I sullenly miss it. I'm standing in front of the gate, my arms full of grocery bags, feeling my stomach pitch to the ground. Nathan reaches out for the bags, but I set them down instead of handing them over. And stand there.

"Hello," he says, unsmiling.

"Hello," I say back.

I saw them fighting once—the actress and her husband. They were out in front of their house, alone, facing each other and speaking quietly, but I could tell they were both terribly upset. I passed by. Looked at her face, facing me. Skin a bit red, splotchy even, but not unattractive the way a normal human's face would be. She just looked flushed with emotion, pretty. Of course.

We stand frozen, facing each other at the stoop. A squat middle-aged woman leads a group of disabled adults by. Some of them stumble, some weave left and right; others walk carefully in a straight line. One man's face is twisted— in agony or not. "Come on, you guys," the leader says cheerfully. "Almost there!" One of them moans and for a second I think I may have made that sound myself.

"Can I come up?" Nathan asks. Sharply. Not really asking. I shake my head. He sighs and lets his hands and head drop. "What is it, what do you want from me?" he asks the steps. "Nothing," I say. He looks back up.

There's a buzzing in my ears during the conversation that follows. I can't hear his words or my own. They resolve into a distant drone. I can't have this, you can't have that, blah blah blah. We've done this before. A million times! Blah blah blah blah blah blah blah blah blah.

Goddamn Mrs. H, who rarely leaves her own stoop, shuffles by. Taking a conveniently timed "walk," though you can hardly call it walking. There's a lull in our dull roar, and Mrs. H sidles in. "How are *you?*" she asks Nathan pointedly. He nods, friendly and animated all of a sudden. Public Nathan. Popular Nathan. He stands and walks down the steps toward her, which is also toward *me*. I shrink back. "I'm fine, Mrs. H. How are you?" he asks warmly. Darling Nathan. Friendly and fun-loving Nathan. "Where've you been?" she asks point-blank. Not buying his shit. I'm surprised. I lean forward eagerly. What will he say? "Oh, I've been around," he says lamely. Mrs. H sees me roll my eyes.

Mrs. H looks from one to the other of us. Like she can see what's left of our shared life: the sadly deflating balloon between him and me. It's not all the way flat, but it's on its way there. I can hear the air hissing out, *looooooooooooooosing.*

Nathan says brightly, "Good to see you, Mrs. H. Take care." What he means is: *Get moving, old lady.* She does. I'd forgotten how nice it is to have a man around for occasions like this—to end awkward conversations, slam the door, or give old ladies the boot without feeling some inconvenient pang of conscience. As much as I despise Mrs. H, I can't help being polite to her, backing slowly away from her, or is that someone else I'm thinking of? My old self? Or someone else entirely? A calmer, kinder, happier person, the woman Nathan thinks he will find, now that I'm out of the way.

After Mrs. H has left, the scene belongs to us again: to Nathan and me. Like the first time we met. On a packed train. We were pressed awkwardly against one another by the bodies around us. Our clothes and skin were damp from the warm city rain outside. We smiled at each other. Or: he smiled and I smiled back. Then the bodies pulled away from us, out of the doors, but we stayed where we were. Straphanging. Lolling our heads. He said, "Where are you heading?" And that was the start.

Or: we met at school. I made eyes at him in poetry class. We were college sweethearts. Held hands on campus, marched side by side for political causes, carried home-made signs with our passively held strident beliefs. NO WAR. NO NUKES. PRO-CHOICE. TAKE BACK THE NIGHT. After the first time we made love, I stole his jeans and wore them with the waist rolled down. We talked nonstop over steaming cups of coffee at the local diner. We were serious, earnest, impassioned, ready to Change The World. He lay under blankets on his bed, recovering from the flu, while I read Donne's sonnets out loud. He said, "Stop it, you're making me sicker." We tipped our heads back in the rain and laughed openmouthed. We got drunk and went streaking. We fucked as quietly as we could in his dorm room, right across from his sleeping roommate. We were young and dumb and madly in love!

Or: we met on the street. Two junkies looking for a fix. Or he ran a lemonade stand in our neighborhood, when we were kids; I paid twenty-five cents for a cup of Crystal Light and eternal love. Or we went Shakespeare and star-crossed—eloped, got married in the dark back room of a neighborhood church, surrounded by rapidly melting candles. When things went sour, he killed himself, and when I woke up I killed myself, too. It all sounds exceedingly better than what I actually got. Here it is, what I got, right fat in front of me.

"Hello," he says, waving his hand in front of my face. "You there?" Then he lifts his shapely, strong hands in the air to say, *What the fuck?* "What are we going to do about this?" he asks. "What?" I ask. Still lost in our fantasy origin stories, none of which are true: we met at a mutual friend's housewarming party in grad school, drunkenly hooked up, and went on predictably from there.

Nathan opens his mouth and there's more buzzing. He stands there buzzing like a bee. He's a giant bee, my soon-to-be-ex-husband, hands on his hips (do bees have hips?), buzzing angrily. It goes on for a while. I have no idea what he's said by the time he finishes and buzzes away. When he finally disappears up the block, swinging his arms forcefully the way he does, I collect my grocery bags and climb the steps to my house.

I was always able to see Nathan coming from far away, regardless of how many other brown-haired handsome-men-of-a-certain-age-with-black-glasses were on the street at the same time. His walk was so distinctive—with his jaunty step and arm-swinging—that I could pick him out instantly. I'd feel a little pang of joy in my chest: here was Nathan, on his way home to me. And now? *There goes Nathan, farther and farther away.*

Back upstairs I feel like I've run a marathon, though I only stood there for a handful of minutes, listening to something that sounded, at times, like the sea. Cat winds around my legs, meowing quietly. I pick her up, crush her to me, rub my face on the back of her head. How she purrs! When I drop her, she lands on her feet, just as she should. Perfect. I will never give her up.

*

Even days after Nathan's surprise attack, I feel like everything inside me has scattered. In class, I grasp at words and
ideas and nothing comes, nothing coheres. I keep pacing,
as if that alone will prove my energy, focus, and author-
ity, but my students watch me like I might be deranged.
Bernardo in particular tracks my movements with his dark
eyes. I'm trying to talk about John Donne's "Batter my
heart, three-person'd God," but all that comes out of my
mouth is trash. Finally, I give up and tell them the poem is
smut, even though I don't really mean it. "It's perverse, this
speaker's lust for God," I say. "His desire to be 'ravished' by
God. Do you know what 'ravished' means?" Know-It-All
Joanne raises her hand. "It means raped," she says flatly.
The class stirs. Devon says, "Why does he want God to
rape him?" Quiet titters around him. "I'm serious," he says,
frowning. Joanne sighs. When she raises her hand again, I
consider not calling on her for a moment, but in the end I
do. There can be no ignoring of students in a class of seven.
"Why is John Donne's poem smut when Emily Dickinson's
poems aren't?" she asks, with that frown on her face. I'm
reduced almost to tears at the thought of Dickinson as
smut, and . . . who is Joanne to ask me anything at all? But
who am *I*, when it comes down to it? I'm not the actress.
I'm nobody, who are you?—ha! "It's totally different," I say

curtly. I see the look in Joanne's eyes, like she's heard the scary tone in my voice and won't push me. Not tonight. Devon keeps his mouth shut, too, though I'm sure he still wants an answer to his question. I simply don't have it in me to give him one.

Bernardo lingers after class. He seems different—even more intense than usual. He comes right to the edge of my desk and reaches out to lightly touch my arm. The first time anyone in the class has touched me. "Are you all right?" I look up at him and say, "No, I'm not." When he suggests going for a drink, I think he's surprised when I say, "Okay."

*

In the morning I go for a long, rambling walk. Past storefronts and restaurants hoisting up their metal shields for the day. Past derelicts begging for change. Past the elderly, walking their elderly dogs. Past children secured to a rope, herded along by frazzled, frowning caretakers. Past strollers, past couples of all kinds carrying out successful adult relationships right here on the street, even despite the relentless passage of time and the crushing baggage of work and . . . life. Last night I nearly fucked my student, or: last night I nearly let my student fuck me.

Ravish me, he whispered up close in my ear at the bar. I could feel his smile in the tiny hairs on my earlobe, and all through the hairlike filigrees of every nerve in my body.

When we left the bar, we stood under the streetlamp, blinking. There I was, with my bleached-out face, my faded lipstick, red-veined dry eyes, and the graying part in my hair I haven't bothered to color in weeks. Bernardo, by contrast, looked tender and young, his face full of color like a succulent fruit. He kept his dark eyes fixed on mine. I took a step back, away from him and out of the glaring light. "Professor—" he said, even though he'd been using my first name at the bar. He stepped toward me. I felt the magnetized pull of his body but at the last moment tore myself away. Silence behind me as I walked quickly into the darkness. I imagined him posing under the streetlamp, staring sulkily after me.

I am sick to death of men. Buzzing, angry men. Hot liquid men. Men wanting sex. Men wanting to touch and be touched. Men wanting to drain you of every last ounce of energy you've reserved for getting through the days. Men under streetlamps, men on my stoop. Men fucking someone against my very gate. Men leaving their refuse everywhere: inside, outside, all over the world. Until the world fills up and spills over as it may soon do: The End.

It's the actress who calms me, of course. Wearing a pink silken robe cinched tightly at the waist, she walks through the dark house turning on one light after another. Each bulb illuminates the soft hills and hollows of her face. *THERE IS SOMEONE IN YOUR HOUSE*, I want to tell her, but I relish the suspense of it, relish knowing something *she*, even *she*, doesn't know, feeling all the more achingly how beautiful she is, how bare her long, curved neck is, until the man steps out of the shadows behind her and I scream.

It's a high-pitched, blood-curdling scream that goes on and on. I have no desire to stop it—it scrapes all the crud out of me from the bottom up. Cat rears back, preparing to hiss. If anyone lived below me, they would come pounding at the door, they would call the police. But no one is there. So I let the scream go on, even after the black-gloved hand clamps over the actress's mouth and her green eyes go wide and glittery.

I wake the next morning refreshed, as if the scream has fully cleansed me. I *didn't* fuck Bernardo, after all—I only *almost* did. I thought about it. And who wouldn't? I'm human, after all.

*

My nerves return just in time for the next class. As I push open the door, I tell myself: *It was nothing. I've done nothing wrong. And besides,* I'm *the grown-up,* I'm *in charge.* The lights are too bright. The students sit in clumps, chattering. They lower their voices when I enter the room. Bernardo sits apart from the others, his legs spread wide. He's wearing frayed jeans and a long-sleeved white button-down shirt with the sleeves rolled up. Loose collar. Dark eyes. The hint of a smile. Beneath it I can see the pain of rejection, and his beauty paired with this new vulnerability takes my breath away. My teacher-mask slips, but I push it on firmly, take a deep breath, turn to the board and write: *SYLVIA PLATH: 1932–1963.*

I clear my throat. "All right, everyone, you should have read 'Ariel,' 'Lady Lazarus,' and 'Fever 103°,' right?" My voice is steady. Professorial. Projecting just loudly enough. I feel a surge of confidence, the way Plath must have felt when these poems came pouring out of her onto the page. Pre-head-in-oven Plath. "Choose one of the poems and write a response. Focus on at least two of the poetic elements we've been discussing this semester—rhyme, meter, imagery, metaphor, line breaks, metonymy, alliteration—and how they combine to convey what you see as the poem's theme, or *one* of the poem's themes. I'll give you twenty minutes." That was fine. I breathe in deeply through my nose—not looking at Bernardo—and out through my mouth as I was taught to do in yoga. I'll have them share their work with a small group, and then discuss as a class. The night will proceed smoothly. I'm in control. I can win.

Circling the room, I try not to stare too closely at Bernardo, who sits quiet and pensive, staring at his blank paper with pen in hand. His lush skin seems to be steaming under the lights. How does he manage to stay quiet and seated, wearing that skin? How have I managed to teach him for all these weeks without marching over to straddle his lap? *Shhhhh*, calm down. Walk away. Look at the wall. Or at Joanne, scratching away at her Plath response. She must be in heaven, letting out the fury I can sense simmering inside her all the time.

After Simon has asked me Stupid Question Number Thirty-Two about Plath, after Joanne has given me countless stern looks and one sisterly nod during our discussion of the suicidal imagery in "Ariel," after Chloe has waved, friendly and shy as always, and closed the door politely behind her: Bernardo stays. I make a show of fussing with my papers. The Bernardo I thought I knew, the class clown, joking and earnest and sweet, teasing me about Diet Cokes and wedding rings, is long gone—replaced by this silently demanding Heathcliff-esque presence. He sits there, legs spread, frowning moodily, leaning his head on his hand while I pack my bag. When he sees I'm done and ready to leave, he comes to life, sliding around the arm of his desk to stand in my way like a petulant boy. I look at his lean, muscular arms, his firm chest. Not a petulant boy: a smoldering, petulant *man*.

But this is a farce. A single woman's fantasy. A scene from *Outlander* or *Fifty Shades of Grey*—or even *Finely Tuned*, the actress's indie romance about a piano teacher whose much younger pupil seduces her. This isn't real—it *cannot* be real. I push him gently aside (my fingers don't burn when they touch his arm—a miracle!) and step to the door, trembling all over but hoping he can't see it. If he were real, wouldn't he speak? Say, "Hey, Professor, wait," or something equally disarming? But he's silent behind me, and doesn't come after me. Was he there at all? When I look behind me before stepping into the elevator, all I see is the empty hall.

I've done it. I've turned the page. There's a plain white sheet before me now. Unblemished. Untouched. In this one small region of my life, I'm starting anew. Back home, I breathe my relief right into Cat's hovering face. She blinks once and licks my nose.

*

I walk briskly into class the next week wearing low heels, black pants, a pale gray silk blouse, and a dark gray suit jacket, with a simple silver locket clasped around my neck: respectable middle-aged women's armor. My outfit mirrors the one the actress wore to teach in every single scene of *Working Class*, in which she inspired tough but tenderhearted community college students to be their best selves—but I doubt my students will catch the reference. It helps me feel powerful and steady, though. I arrange my things on the desk, and begin: "Let's look at Wanda Coleman's *American Sonnets* in your course packet. Look at number ten first. Read it over to yourselves, then jot down some ideas about why you think Coleman would use the sonnet form to write about the legacy of slavery in this country. Consider what we've learned about sonnets in your answer—their technical features, history, and the key practitioners of the form—and then discuss what you've written with a partner, or in a small group." I'm peering around the room, letting my eyes rest sternly but fleetingly on each student: Chloe, James, Mary, Joanne, Simon, Devon . . . everyone but Bernardo is here.

He strides in late. Saunters to his desk. *Saunter, saunter, saunter.* I'm in the midst of responding to James's comment about Coleman's use of enjambment when Bernardo finds the desk with the creaky chair and sits down noisily in it. I don't look. His eyes are on me, weighing me down, but

I don't look. And don't look and don't look until finally, I force myself to look. I hold his eyes for a moment without interrupting the flow of my talk. I let my eyes wander casually away from his. I gesture excitedly with my hands. I laugh, and the students laugh with me. I lead them to the brilliant conclusion that Coleman subverts the historically white, Western sonnet by using it to write about slavery and also by flouting conventions of the form. They're with me! All of them, that is, except for Bernardo: the black hole whose gravitational field I've just escaped. But do black holes resent the planets and space debris that spin out of reach? Bernardo certainly seems to. He sits there, emanating dark matter, pulling at me with his liquid eyes. I don't care. I resist.

After class, he lingers again. He sits there, silent and insolent, while I gather my bags and ignore him. "You look thirsty, Professor," he says at last. I can almost hear his saucy grin. I don't respond. I *am* thirsty. I pick up my bottled water, open the cap, tip my head all the way back, and swallow it down. I show him the soft pale white of my throat. Set the drained bottle down on my desk with a thunk. That's that. He sits there looking stunned as I exit.

I could tap dance down the street. But I don't. I'm a pulsing, strutting power field funneled into the quiet figure of a woman walking home from work, alone and virtuous.

Mrs. H stops me as I pass her gate. It's late for her—it takes me by surprise to see her haunting the stoop at this hour. "The block party's coming soon," she says by way of greeting. "October fifteenth." "Yes, I got the e-mail," I say. She gives me a nod. "You going?" I'm sweating in my actress-inspired teacher clothes. I want to go home and take them off, then jump in the shower. *Of course I'm going, old lady, what else do I have to do?* "Yes," I say, starting to move away. "Alone?" she asks, trying to hold my eyes. The power I felt just a moment ago, striding along after my victorious performance in class, starts to shrivel. "Yes," I say, defeated. She nods and smiles widely, satisfied.

When I get home, I call to Cat but she doesn't come. I peel open a can of her favorite food—liver and chicken hearts—and still she doesn't come. I check all the rooms and get down on my hands and knees to look under the bed, the dresser, the couch. My heart starts beating hard—"Cat!" I call frantically. "Caaaatttt!" I wail. I stand in the middle of the living room, sweaty and wild-eyed, imagining Nathan sneaking in here somehow to grab Cat. That bastard! Panic turns to rage. I rustle through my teaching bag for my phone. Bastard. I'll get him for this. Then I hear a tiny *mew* from the extra room.

When I step inside, I see the shiny bike I stole and the box full of screenplays I practically yanked from my neighbor's grasp. This is my walk-in showcase of trophies, of triumphs. But it also holds remnants of the old, imagined life I once dreamed I'd have, the one whose aura pricks me like the tiny needles I used to use for IVF prep. I push through the tickling pain to find Cat in a wardrobe stuffed with old linens. "Oh, Cat," I say. "Cat." Rubbing my face against hers as she purrs. She had gotten herself wedged in the back of the wardrobe somehow. *Oh, Cat.* I take her to the kitchen and watch her feast.

There is no door to that room, so I seal it off with duct tape to make a kind of wall. But I still know it's there—and so does Cat. She stands where the doorway used to be and meows. I scoot her away gently with my foot, but she always comes back to the spot. She sits down, slowly, like a tired queen, and gives herself a postprandial bath.

I've found an old curtain to hang over the taped-up doorway. Cat watches me warily as I bang the hanging fabric in place with hammer and nails. When I'm done, she sniffs at it, then ducks right under and sits in the dark space between it and the tape wall. I can just see her white paws below the hem of the curtain, and sometimes the black tip of her twitching tail.

*

Bernardo comes to the next class looking dejected, and noticeably less intense. He hardly meets my eyes. I feel generosity toward him swell inside me, and give his downcast face a particularly warm smile. His eyes flutter up and hold mine.

Tonight is our poetry workshop, the first of only two we'll have. I ask everyone to get out their original poems and pass copies around. The room fills with the productive sound of paper shuffling overlaid with light, anxious chatter. "Mine sucks," Simon says loudly, and it's probably true. As far as I know, they will all "suck," but I'll have to take each one as seriously as a masterwork.

It always seems like a fun idea, when I'm in the class-planning phase, to add a day or two of workshop to the syllabus. Give students the chance to be creative, let them see what it's like to be on the "other side." The difficulty comes when *I* have to try out the other side, too, and act like a teaching poet, one who knows how to gently, professionally, confidently critique student poems—even atrocious ones. *I don't know what I'm doing!* I want to shout. *Sure, I studied the greats, but I only took one lousy poetry workshop in grad school!* When I open my mouth to speak, there's a voice in my head going, *Horseshit horseshit horseshit*, at the words that eventually sputter out.

But not tonight. Tonight the words come flowing out of me like I'm the actress in *Working Class*, standing at the helm— or the whiteboard—of class, leading her underprivileged students to enlightenment and gainful employment one transcendent word at a time. Of course, they don't have frills like poetry workshop in *Working Class*. Still: tonight I somehow know the perfect thing to say at every turn.

"Joanne, your line breaks aren't moving the poem forward. There's a narrative here—a really compelling one—but it's weighed down by those overlong lines."

"Don't be afraid to use three-syllable words like this, Devon. But use them sparingly. You've broken the rhythm here, it was moving right along but here it breaks. Don't sacrifice sound for ten-dollar words!" (Appreciative laughter from students.)

I lead them around by their noses, offer them insights like bread and wine. I'm the expert, the scholar, the tough-but-warm mentor. They are mine tonight, these students, every one. Even Bernardo has raised his eyes to join in the communal glow. His poem is up next. He must not have sent his around earlier—now the copies pass from hand to hand.

First I see Mary's eyebrows go up. Then Joanne's. Then: there's a roomful of raised eyebrows. Eyes glued to the page before each of them.

Dear Ms. X, it reads. All I can do is scan and catch words. *After class. Warm thigh. Mine. Lips. Gasp. Tangled. Divine.* I clear my throat. "Bernardo, could you read this aloud please?" I say, trying so hard to sound calm and controlled that I veer into something like an imitation of an English schoolmarm.

I must be the color of a red sheet. A hot sweaty red satin bedsheet.

"Dear Ms. X," Bernardo starts in his husky voice. Then he looks up. Looks right at me and *recites*. "Last night after class, when your warm thigh pressed / against mine / when our lips touched the rims / of our glasses at just the same time / I felt an internal gasp / as did you, and later / our arms and legs tangled, breaths mingled, souls touched . . . / and it was divine."

After a beat I clear my throat and say, "Thank you, Bernardo. Everyone, take three minutes to make notes on the poem." I lean over the desk, pen in hand. All business on the outside—all chaos and heat and sinking wreckage within.

It's dead silent as everyone bends their heads to read. I can't do anything but stare at the wall clock and watch the second hand move. It moves, and moves, and moves past the two-minute mark. On to the three-minute mark. And beyond. People start to shift, rustle their papers. Joanne clears her throat as if to say, *Professor?*

Why in god's name can't I channel the actress's "Professor T" from *Working Class* now? I see her pacing back and forth, lecturing and fielding sporadic questions, as teachers always do in movies. But Professor T never had to contend with one of her students writing a sex poem about her. Of course, Professor T would never have gone to the bar with Bernardo in the first place.

Finally, I look down at the page. Crinkle my brow as if reading so deeply and critically that I cannot be disturbed. It's a god-awful poem—at least there's that. I stare hard at the words. Nearly grunt at one of the clumsiest line breaks and something trips, or slips, into place inside me. *Oh, Bernardo. You shouldn't have crossed me.* I almost scribble that down on the page as my ultimate note but instead I write: *Good attempt at erotic poetry. You should read some Pablo Neruda, Sharon Olds, Audre Lorde, and Sappho for superior examples.* I've become crisp and businesslike. My cheeks have cooled to ash.

When I glance up, I see them all staring at me. Pens down. Waiting. I start to feel myself slipping again. "Well," I start shakily. "It's a good—a nice erotic poem." Bernardo's lips twitch into a half smirk. He's got me. I'm going down. The thought sends something scrambling in me—little fingernails gaining foothold in the crumbling brick of an old well—and I rally. "I appreciate the use of slant rhyme, but even though it's not exact, it becomes overwhelming. It makes the poem singsongy, not sexual, not a poem about two aroused adults." Oh how the words come tumbling out! How I wish I could kiss each one as it leaves my lips! There's a love poem for you. "What do the rest of you think? Any ideas for how to improve this first draft?"

My eyes flit over Bernardo's face. He's stunned, I can tell, and looks to his fellow students for help. The fool—he expects them to come to the aid of his sad little poem. They don't. They tear it apart like dogs would a carcass. They've been waiting for this. It's what I've told them not to do, *never* to do, in a workshop. This tearing and splitting and patching together. But tonight I let them at it.

When we finish, the marked-up drafts pile up on Bernardo's desk like broken limbs and bullet wounds after a battle. It seems almost superfluous to continue, but I move on quickly to the next student poem, and the one after that. It's my duty, after all.

I stop in front of the actress's house after class: the husband slouches at the table in sweats, eating yogurt; the actress is nowhere in sight. Is she reading upstairs? Asleep with the baby? There's someone at the stove, cleaning up—the cook? I feel certain I've had more excitement tonight than they have, and the thought warms me, lights me up. *Little star, glowing bright*, I think, smiling to myself.

*

I hear nothing from Nathan. He's given up! Victory warms my feet in the form of Cat, who drapes herself over the foot of my bed at night. She follows me when I get up to pee in the middle of the night, and then leaps into my lap while I sit on the toilet. She never did this before. Cat kneads the tops of my thighs with her delicate paws and then settles down, purring contentedly. I pull her close and rub my face against the back of her head. How sweet she is, how tender! Why did it take me so long to appreciate her? She's a darling, my Cat.

My phone rings so seldom now that it startles me when it does. I'm curled in a corner of the couch early the next morning with a coffee mug, still feeling satisfied about how I handled last night's class, when the phone jumps to life. I jump with it. And don't answer—of course. I just look at the screen. It says: *Unknown Number*. Hmph. Not Nathan, then. Whew. I let it shimmy and shake on the table beside me until it ends, then wait to see if there's a message. There is.

"This is Sandy Hodder of Platz, Hodder, and Wright. I'm calling on behalf of my client, Nathan Fielding. He has initiated divorce proceedings and would like to set up a meeting with you and your attorney next week to discuss the division of your property and belongings—including the cat."

She says the last part wryly, like she's holding back a laugh. Like she can't believe the shit her clients get into with their pathetic ex-spouses. Suddenly, Cat yowls and leaps from the couch. I'd been rubbing her softly, but then I must have clutched. Clutched her fur and pulled. Though I don't remember doing it.

My hands are shaking—I've had to set my coffee mug down. The awful dread that filled my stomach in the early days after Nathan left settles inside me once again. Divorce. The finality of it, delivered via an absolute stranger, a *lawyer*, quietly mocking me for clinging to my ex-husband's cat. Would the actress allow herself to be treated this way? Never. Before long I'm sobbing, leaking snot, letting it all come out. I'd thought the whole Nathan ordeal was over, that I'd won—what a fool I've been.

When I'm able to lift myself creakily from the couch, still sniffling but mostly composed, I do the only thing I know to do anymore: I walk. Sure enough, just as I leave my house in my splotchy-faced, bleary-eyed state, the actress walks by. Fresh from the masseuse, or the spa, or a fancy breakfast somewhere, her face glowing with comfort, satisfaction, and health, dressed in a dove-gray linen jumpsuit that would look ridiculous on anyone else—on her it looks divine. *She* is divine. As she passes by she gives me a tight smile. I can smell the perfume she wears—just the right amount, not the old-lady-on-the-train fragrance cloud that makes you gag. This scent makes me lift my nose in the air and turn my head after her like a dog. No one could ever not know she's a star. One of the golden ones. My mouth fills with saliva, or saliva mixed with something else, something viscous. I lean my head down to spit. It lands right on a pile of dog shit. Looking down, I feel nausea rise to the back of my throat. I feel like I just leaned down and licked the turds, instead of spitting on them from a distance. I feel like they've been shoved down my throat.

Without realizing it, I've headed for the park. I haven't been here in ages, and as soon as I pass through the archway that marks the entrance, I remember why. It's early enough that the central meadows are free of older children playing soccer or baseball and flying kites, but . . . the babies are out. The mothers and babies, the nannies and babies (mostly the nannies and babies): babies everywhere. Mewling in strollers, stretching chubby arms toward their caretakers, crawling on the filthy rubberized ground of the toddler playground. I try not to look. I try not to see their plump hands grasping chalk, try to shut out their small cries of delight, try not to watch the mother nursing her babe on the bench, in the shade.

I imagined heaviness in my breasts, the heaviness of milk, when I thought I was pregnant once. Months and months ago. My period was a few days late and I convinced myself— or *almost* convinced myself—that the blue veins I could see through the skin of my breasts were darkening, that my nipples were enlarging as all the guides said they would, that when I cupped my breasts in my hands they felt heavy and milk-filled. What animal pleasure! What idiocy! I'd stand and stare in the mirror at those veins, checking the spider veins on my thighs, even, for a sign that they, too, were changing. I thought, *Finally, it's happening, I'm going to push a child's head against my breasts and feel it pull down on my nipple to feed. At last!*

And then I started to bleed. I hadn't told Nathan that time, thank god. There'd been other close calls, other failures, and each time was like punching him in the face. I loved him, so I couldn't bear to see him hurt. Or maybe I couldn't bear to remind him it was all because of me—my wreck of a body. It didn't matter, ultimately, what I did or didn't tell him—he figured it out.

I stare at the nursing woman. At the plump curve of her breast rising over the babe's head as it pulls and sucks, drawing the milk down into its little body to grow bigger and stronger. I've seen it happen! I've watched the children on our block grow from seedlings to squirts to full-grown *people*. It amazes me. And yet I feel repulsed, too. If I could suckle a child myself, would I feel the same? Maternally virtuous, like I was growing a future citizen of the nation, but simultaneously disgusted and trapped, clamoring to be free from the leech at my breast?

*

I return home, exhausted and emptied out. Fitting my key in the lock, a wave of absolute terror washes over me: this is where my phone and computer live. This is how all the poisonous others reach me, infect me, ruin my days. But what can I do? Camp out in the hall with Cat? Take over the first-floor entryway? Winter is coming. It's not even practical. I sigh, turn the key, and go in.

Despite that initial jolt of fear, I head straight for my phone and laptop as soon as I'm through the door. This is why I'm easily polluted. Nothing new on the phone, but there's a message from Bernardo in my inbox, with the subject heading in all caps: POEM REVISION. I stare at it in the list of new e-mails, willing it to go away. I could always just select it and hit Delete, but I can't. I can't not read this e-mail.

> Hi Professor, thought I'd revise my poem after the comments I received in workshop. Thanks for any feedback on this. Bernardo.

I'm grimacing as I scan the lines.

> Dear Ms. X, Last night after class, / when your wet hot tongue / singed mine, when your wet hot / tongue touched my cock, / I sighed. But later I / gasped, feeling all of you / all the way inside, slipping / in and out of that deep, dark place / where the two of us lie. It was / and is / divine.

What is Bernardo doing? What is he *thinking*? Playing with his fate in my class—no, in *school*—in this way? What a fool! I try to hold on to the anger, but the images start to take shape. Dammit. I push Cat off the bed rudely, like I used to do, ignoring her yowl, and work myself to orgasm as quickly as I can.

> Dear Bernardo, This is quite a rewrite. I don't think it addresses your classmates' concerns that the poem is "purple"—that was the word Joanne used, I believe. It seems to have grown more purple yet in the revision process, and more graphic. Erotic poetry doesn't have to be graphic, you know; it can be more powerful when the lines and images are subtle, suggestive, rather than overtly sexual. You may want to set this one aside. I'll let you turn in a different one for a grade, if you like.

I was only able to write the message after I'd washed my hands and splashed cool water on my face and neck. By then my heart had relaxed back to its normal pace, and I could pretend that the poem had nothing to do with me, nothing to do with the night Bernardo and I went to the bar, that it was just the ordinary nuisance of a bad student poem. *This piece of trash has nothing to do with me—nothing at all!* Just as I'm letting those words sink in, the doorbell sounds. I press the button and hear Mrs. H say, without any preamble, "Can I ask you something?" Oh god.

Instead of buzzing her in and making her struggle up the stairs, which would be gratifying but would also allow her to glimpse the inside of my apartment, I walk down and open the front door. I've pasted a smile on my face. "What's up, Mrs. H?" I ask. She doesn't smile back. She's wearing some sort of blue-and-yellow-striped muumuu that hurts my eyes to look at. Can't she see how the bright colors clash with her faded old skin? "You haven't responded to the block party e-mails," she says. "Can you help with setup this year? I know you're alone, but . . ." Her eyes flit beyond me, to the dim hall. There's nothing to see there—just the common staircase and the cracked floor tiles—but still I shift a little to block her view. "Of course I am! I'll come down at what, nine a.m.?" I ask in my cheerful voice. "Eight thirty," she says. "Sharp." She's already turning away. That's all she wanted, but I feel a sudden urge for more. "Mrs. H," I call after her. "Do you think the weather will be good?" As if she—or anyone—could know this far in advance. "It doesn't matter," she says, shrugging her shoulders. "We'll have it rain or shine. Always do." Then she walks slowly down the stoop, one step at a time, sideways, clutching the rail, and toddles back to her house.

Mrs. H has given me something new to think about: the block party. I latch onto it and don't let my mind wander into other, more troubling areas. The party is still two and a half weeks away, but it isn't too early to get organized. This year it feels even more potentially momentous than ever before: *I will talk to the actress, befriend her, utterly charm her.* I sit down at the kitchen table to make a list: *one small watermelon, 1 lb. orzo, fresh basil, feta cheese, case of beer, good bread?* It seems inadequate, especially compared to the exotic dishes the actress will bring: Wilted escarole and quinoa. Apple-cider-braised root vegetables. Farro salad with dried cherries and hazelnuts.

The words alone galvanize me. I soon find myself standing in front of the glass case at City Pantry, staring at a selection of vibrant and healthy foods I barely recognize. *I could shop here for the block party, too.* Not now, of course, but on the morning of. I could break with tradition and splurge, and then she and I would hold up our bags, point and laugh. Instant conversation starter. Worth it, for the giant hole in my paycheck? While I'm pondering the pros and cons, the clerk waits behind the case, looking expectantly at me. After a while he clears his throat. I keep staring, lost in all the colors and descriptions, unable to speak, to say, *I'm just looking*, politely. Eventually he wanders off, though I can still feel his eyes on me. Crushed new potatoes with extra virgin olive oil. Chickpea and couscous salad with chermoula. All of it fifteen dollars per pound. At the end of what feels like an hour, I turn and walk out.

After coming back from City Pantry, I pause for a moment on the stoop. It's nice out. Warm but with a cool breeze, so I sit on the top step to smoke. No one I know comes by; it's like I'm invisible up here, lifted above the street, apart from the flow of the city but still part of its fabric. I realize, somewhere in the back of my mind, that the actress could come by, but I don't long for it to happen the way I usually do. Maybe it's the relative nearness of the block party. I want to save up and see her *there*, in full view, with full access at last. My troubles with Nathan and Bernardo seem far away now, minuscule and harmless, like objects seen through a telescope, though not pretty like stars. Breathing the delicious smoke in and out, I feel as if I've always been here and always will be.

But when I return upstairs, I instantly succumb to that constant, subconscious itch: I check my e-mail, pretending to myself that I want to review the details of the block party setup. Bernardo hasn't responded. I sag against the back of my chair, partly relieved, partly annoyed. I have to keep myself from poking him with another e-mail—a desperate move. In order to maintain the upper hand, I *cannot* be desperate. I must be cool, professorial.

It's 7 p.m.: still no answer from Bernardo. *Cool, professorial,* I tell myself, breathing in through the nose, out through the mouth. Does he work? I seem to remember he doesn't. That he's independently wealthy or something. Entitled rich boy—thinks he can ignore my gently disguised commands and get away with it. I resist the urge to read the revised poem again, afraid it will send me back to the couch.

Midnight: NO ANSWER. Who does he think he is?

The e-mail arrives when I least expect it: six the next morning. I am already awake, staring blearily at the screen, when it pops into view.

> Dear Professor, thank you for your insights. I do not understand "purple" and did not understand it when Joanne said it, either. What is "purple"? Is it because the poem is about sex? You have always told us that poetry is a space free of judgment and censorship. Perhaps we can discuss this after the next class? ☺ I'll buy the first round. Bernardo

I'll buy the first round. Wow. His impertinence drives me to hit Reply and type:

> Purple means it is over-the-top, excessive, outrageous, and poorly written. Too many adjectives, too much emotion, too much gratuitous sex. I would appreciate it if you

would simply take my critique as it should be taken: as wise words from *your professor*. Now do the work: write a new poem or revise this one carefully, and turn in your final version to me in class.

There. The final word. I'm proud of myself for not responding to the drinks invite—except indirectly, by italicizing *your professor*. A subtle show of strength: *I'm* in charge, you idiot. I hit Send and then read back through the entire thread, beginning with his note about the revision. My heartbeat spikes when I get to the revised poem:

Dear Ms. X, / Last night after class, when your warm thigh pressed / against mine / when our lips touched the rims / of our glasses at just the same time / I heard you gasp / like the sound you made when our / arms and legs tangled / in sweat-drenched sheets / breaths mingling / souls touching / when we reached out and grasped the divine.

What? Where was the poem I'd read earlier today? I scroll through the exchange, searching for the word *cock*, but it isn't there. I even do a Search and Find, my fingers shaking. Nothing. *Cock* isn't there. The version I read has vanished, replaced with this anodyne rewrite. *Where had the dirtier poem gone?* Into the ether, with all of the other things I've lost.

*

Though I've coaxed a shell of calm superiority into place, it utterly crumbles when I step into the classroom and see Bernardo. It's as if everyone can see me masturbating on the couch to his erotic poem—the one that apparently didn't exist—gasping my final satisfaction. His mouth opens as if he might speak. I give him a severe look that says, *Quiet*, and he shuts his mouth again—like an obedient fish. But as I'm reaching into my bag, pulling out books, pens, and stapled copies I've made for today's discussion on postwar collage poetry, Bernardo slides around his desk, comes up to me, and clears his throat. When he talks it's low, so hushed in fact that I have to lean close to hear him. "I'm sorry, Professor. I didn't mean to be disrespectful. I just didn't understand what you meant. Honestly. Poetry's hard for me." I'm looking in his eyes the whole time but I can *smell* his sincerity—it's the smell of his nervous sweat, a sharp, masculine scent that makes my nipples harden. I wonder momentarily if he can see them, my outsized pink nipples, poking at him through the thin material of my fussy silk blouse. I haven't said a word yet; I've tried to keep my gaze cool and distant, but he must sense some kind of give in me—he smiles and starts to relax back into his loose, languorous self. Meanwhile, six pairs of eyes look on, six pairs of ears strain to catch what passes between us. I try to think of *them*, the others, when I respond. "I accept your apology, Bernardo," I say in my sternest teacher's voice. "I know it can be hard to take criticism." He nods solemnly. "I'll do better, Professor," he says, but it sounds half-hearted. Even a little snide? Like he's smirking beneath the show of earnestness. I watch him walk back to his desk and take his seat.

Bernardo keeps his deep brown eyes on me all night—not apologetically or carefully or respectfully—but *on me*. Expectant, warm, and electric. Even so, the class runs smoothly. I lecture a bit on the Objectivist poets, introduce them to Lorine Niedecker—one of my personal favorites—and they seem to enjoy it. With each passing moment, I feel returned to my rightful position on the dais that lifts professors up and out of the fray. I *am* Professor T tonight. The students have tilted their heads back so they can see me up here—their eyes fix on mine adoringly, their ears catch my every word, and their hearts beat steadily, *thump thump thump*, so assured are they in my presence, so reassured by my expertise and my handling of any and all awkwardness. Students *need* teachers, just as children need parents, just as I need the actress shining above me, showing me my rightful place in the world. Why, then, do I rail against it sometimes? Tonight, by the end of class, I'm suffused with the warmth of knowing and embracing my rightful place, and the students embrace me back with their eyes as they leave the classroom, one by one, until only Bernardo remains, until only Bernardo's eyes remain locked on mine, unchildlike and burning with a different fire. A fire out of order in the order of things. "Let's get a drink," I say as we gather our notebooks and bags. I can't say why—or what—I'm doing. Bernardo looks taken aback, at first, but then he smiles, shrugs, and says, "Sure."

I lead him to the same bar we visited the other night, down a narrow flight of stairs. He follows me to the back room, which is quiet, dark, and empty. Periodically I try to interrogate myself: when I go to the bathroom, when I wait for Bernardo to come back with our second round of drinks, when we drain the round after that. But my mind is blank. Or is it just deeply calm? I do not know myself tonight. Or: I know myself so deeply and intuitively that there is no need for interrogation, only this placid floating is required. I float on and on.

We talk about his family back in Italy, his studies, and his plans for the future. He asks me nothing about myself, but I prefer it that way. The noise coming from his mouth is like the buzzing noise that Nathan made when we fought on the steps of our brownstone, but this is a soft buzz, a buzz that draws me closer and closer to Bernardo's warm body. After the fourth drink, we leave the bar and head straight for his place.

It isn't like the poem at all. It's awkward at first; I sit stiffly on the couch in his Spartan apartment. Bernardo disappears into what must be the bedroom, leaving me to stare at the blank flat-screen TV for a handful of minutes. Finally he returns and sits down next to me. After a few beats of silence, I pull one of his hands to my breasts. He responds quickly. Opens my blouse and dismantles my bra in several swift moves. In no time at all, his dick is out, I'm sucking it hungrily, he's pushing my head down on it and grunting. Then I'm on my hands and knees and he's gripping my hair and pumping into me from behind and I'm barking—yes, barking!—with pleasure.

And then it's over. "Nothing like the poem at all," I say, and we chuckle. My head is resting on his chest while he smooths my hair. "It happens all the time," I tell him, "students and teachers." As if he doesn't know. "Has it happened to you before?" Bernardo asks, a slight quaver in his voice. "No," I say. "No, I haven't let it." I don't explain why I let it happen this time, and he doesn't ask. The actress wouldn't clarify. Murky is better. We swirl our hands in the warm, murky waters and sleep.

When my eyelids open I know instantly where I am. There's no hazy confusion, no momentary reprieve: I know what I've done. My head pounds. I try to move the bed as little as possible as I rise. Bernardo stirs but doesn't seem to wake—unless he's faking. I hurriedly dress, gather my bag and coat, and sneak out of the apartment like the near criminal I am. Just as I'm letting the door close behind me I hear what I think is someone calling my name, softly and gently as I've always dreamed a lover would. It comes from the inner recesses of the apartment, but not from Bernardo's bedroom. It's plaintive and beautiful; it raises the tiny hairs along my arms, but I shut the door anyway and go.

Once home, I pace the rectangle of my living room rug, holding Cat in my arms like a baby. She lies there, pliant and willing, until she tires of the movement and the feeling of constraint and pushes her back legs against me to leap from my arms. What should I do now? How can I fix this execrable mess? I can't. I simply have to ignore it the best I can.

*

I miss you. Three simple words from Bernardo via text. How does he have my number? Why do I have his? Then I vaguely recall exchanging information over the third or fourth drink, and groan. I set the phone facedown on my bedside table. I don't reply, but I can't help checking the screen now and then. I stare at Bernardo's message until it rouses me—not to masturbate, or text back—but to clean the apartment. To *monster* clean it.

Nathan's the one who called it a "monster clean" first. I never cleaned regularly—he was always after me about it, though he wouldn't do it himself—but every few months or so, I'd scour and organize every inch of our small home, and Nathan would come home, sniffing the air and grinning. "You did it!" he'd say, as if I were a toddler, newly toilet trained, who'd successfully pooped in the potty. Back in those days, I would feel as correspondingly proud as a toddler might, in response to his praise. After a while I stopped including the spare room in my clean—there is doubtless a thick layer of dust covering every surface in there—and then when things went to hell I stopped monster cleaning entirely. Nathan added it to the list of my infractions before he left. As I go about now, red-faced and sweating in an old T-shirt and pajama shorts, unsettling everything, dusting and spraying and polishing, the spare room stays fixed. A shrine. I can't see anything through the tape wall I've put up for Cat, but I know the pink bike glints in there, in the semi-dark, alongside the cardboard boxes full of treasure. Like time capsules full of the old life, the good life, the imagined life I might have had. All of it, the pristine glory of it, mocks me for the irreversible mistake I've just made.

Hey, the next text says. *You there?* A little less plaintive, a little more demanding. I thought maybe he would have given up, had his fling with the professor and moved on, but no, of course not—this is Bernardo: the one who pouts over his bad grade, the one who noticed my missing ring, the one who has practically stalked me this whole semester. What a fool I've been! I don't answer. I go on cleaning. Reversing the passage of time. Making things right. The bathroom now, wiping around the base of the toilet. Erasing the stains of human pollution. *My* pollution, I remind myself. Because I'm the only human left polluting in here.

I decide to cancel the next class. Not yet, but I'm definitely going to cancel it. I can't let the anticipation of it ruin the block party, which is coming up fast. Then, after I've had a break, I'll be able to make a dignified return. Bernardo will be silenced by my wintry stare, by my tightly buttoned blouse. But haven't I tried that before? Haven't I set out to freeze him, only to land in his bed? But next time I'll be firm. It will work. It *has to.*

When I'm done scrubbing grit and mildew from the tiles, I step into a hot shower and let it steam Bernardo and the monster clean right out of my pores. I step out feeling purified. Wholesome, almost. Cat emerges from wherever she was hiding during all the commotion and blinks at me, then mews. *Where is my food?* It's dinnertime.

Bernardo writes: *Really, I miss you. I won't say it again. Come over.*

Later that night: *Please. You know where I live.*

And later still: *Why you being like this?*

And at last: *You came on to me, you know. I didn't even want it. FUCK YOU.*

In the silence that follows his final text, and with the help of several glasses of wine, I gradually achieve a state of inner peace.

I post a message online to cancel the next class. I cite a family death—just like a student would. *My grandmother died. My father is having open-heart surgery. My dog has cancer. I can't cope. Please forgive me. Please give me an extension. I can't focus on schoolwork right now. Please, I beseech you, release me, Professor.* Now it's my turn.

Before me is only: the block party. I stare hard at the party and imagine it, shining and whole, like Yeats's golden-scaled bird of Byzantium hovering just above my horizon. Riding that bird is *the actress*. She will swoop in, bearing bags full of delicacies, and redeem the rotten mess of my life with one swift touch of her bird's wing. I close my eyes to everything else.

*

The day of the block party dawns clear and cool. It's supposed to be warm but not hot by late morning, and sunny all day. We've had block parties threatened by storms, excessive heat, and even a small tornado once, but this one, the one I will attend alone, newly Nathan-stripped, will take place on a perfect jewel of a day. I dress myself accordingly—I want to shine like a perfect jewel, too. I found a stylish sundress, like the actress often wears, at the hipper-than-thou consignment shop down the street. I spent more than an hour there, fumbling through the clothes—arranged idiotically by color, not size—holding my nose because of the dank smell of rot the other shoppers don't seem to mind, until I found it. It's perfect: dark green, sleeveless, with a fitted top and long, swirly skirt. It shows off my full breasts and my trim waist. The waist of a twenty-five-year-old! The breasts of a woman who's never had children! I'll wear my long string of black pearls and matching pearl earrings. Black ballet flats. My hair will be ironed into a sleek, shining bob.

And I'll top it off with my big sunglasses and my trademark lipstick that matches *hers*.

The actress is coming! The actress is coming! echoes inanely in my head as I dress, sending tremors through my fingers as I loop the pearls around my neck. When I step back to admire myself in the mirror, I wonder for a moment if I've overdone it, if my dress outstrips this mundane affair: aluminum trays of homemade food on a Costco folding table, bottles of beer jumbled in with juice boxes in the cooler, Daniel from next door manning the grill, and everyone sweating in T-shirts and shorts, or in simple cotton sundresses and chunky mom-sandals. Oh well. Would *she* worry about being overdressed? Would *she* allow a moment's hesitation for looking better, fancier, more refined than everyone else? Not a chance.

I've abandoned the City Pantry idea and made my water-melon and feta orzo salad; it looks refreshing and delicious. I've bought my twelve-pack of beer, and I've also bought a superb loaf of bread from the local bakery. My apartment may be empty, my bank account may be dwindling, but here I am, fashionably dressed, lightly perfumed, and looking slim and elegant in the mirror. I practice my widest, most confident smile. "No, Nathan and I aren't together anymore," I'll say, holding an imagined interrogator's gaze. "We separated amicably . . . it's fine!"

When I see the bouncy house filling with air, I know it's time to go outside. Mrs. H is already down there, cane in hand, waving it in the air sometimes to emphasize a point or indicate a direction to her willing servants (my neighbors). I'll be joining those fools in just a few moments.

I give Cat an affectionate scratch behind the ears—those soft little ears, pink as shells inside—and close the door.

No one looks up, not even the relentlessly observant Mrs. H, when I step out of the building carrying the glass dish balanced on top of the beer case, bread loaf tucked neatly under my arm. Even in my fabulous dress, with my sparkling smile, I remain invisible to all of them below, scurrying purposefully here and there. For a moment everything inside of me wilts—so much so that I nearly drop my dish. But what else can I do? I jut my chin out defiantly and walk down the stairs.

I'm arranging my food on the table when I feel someone behind me. I turn around and see Mrs. H, breathing heavily like she's speed-hobbled all the way over to me. "You were supposed to help this morning," she practically shouts. Is she going deaf? I realize at once that she's right, that I primped and preened right through my "shift," but I fake righteousness. "No," I say soundly, like I'm talking to a crazed child. "I'm down here *now* because I'm supposed to help *now*, with the food table." I see something waver in the old goon's watery eye—a flicker of self-doubt. Good. She makes a noise in the back of her throat and shuffles away.

I'm the first person to grab a beer from the cooler, at 11:15 a.m. There's been a long, blurred hour of cordially greeting neighbors, receiving bemused compliments on my dress, catering to the older folks, and chuckling at the kids running straight for the bouncy house. I've been eyeing the actress's front door the whole time, hoping—then praying—to see her emerge. What if she's out of town on a shoot? What if they're upstate for the week? My time, my dress, my whole day wasted, and the wreck of my life unsalvageable after all. When the sun is high in the sky and I'm on my third beer and starting to sweat, not from the heat but from the horror of her absence, it happens: she appears, with her two older children in tow. Everyone stays as they were, but everything shifts imperceptibly. The hum of the party quiets a little. No one turns to gawk, but people struggle to maintain the conversations they're in—"What was that, Bill?" "What was I just saying?" They train their eyes on their plastic forks and sagging paper plates, full of wieners and chips and my orzo salad; they take small, nervous sips from the beers in their hands.

In that very moment, I'm caught in conversation with one of the women my age—I don't know her name, I don't know her kids' names, I don't care. We're talking—no, *she's* talking—about the neighborhood school. She assumes I have kids, too—she doesn't even bother to ask. I just play along. I'm a neighborhood mom, just like her, nodding along to her complaints about the principal, the school garden in disrepair, her eldest son's "totally incompetent" teacher. But the whole time, I'm feeling *her* behind me: the exalted one. The actress's daughters skip toward the bouncy house, hand in hand. Mother follows daughters and suddenly she is standing *right next to me*. A moment later she steps lightly away from us, closer to the bouncy house, but still in my line of view. I can see her trim, muscled arms and the curve of her neck below the smooth edge of a new blonde bob. It must be for a role. It suits her—like everything does. She's not wearing a sundress this year. She has on wide linen pants, a sleeveless gold silk shirt, and thong-style sandals. She looks gorgeous, relaxed. Now I feel ridiculous in my extravagant dress and black pearls. But it's too late to go upstairs and change—that would be even *more* ridiculous. I try to stand straighter, try to make my outfit feel like a second skin—the way her outfit looks on *her*.

"Sorry?" I say. The neighborhood mom is asking me something. "What grade is your son in?" she asks, a slight edge to her voice. "Second," I say, without missing a beat. Then I excuse myself and walk away.

It happens by the food table. She hasn't put out any offerings yet, so I've been lingering there, half-heartedly chatting now and then but mostly standing like a sentinel at the dessert end of the table, fourth—fifth?—beer bottle in hand, trying to look welcoming and self-sufficient all at once. I must be ready when she comes. I *will* be ready, I think, swigging my warm beer. Sure enough, she steps out of her house moments later with a large aluminum tray. I feel as though I've orchestrated this moment, as if I've attached myself to her via a thin silken cord, and given it a tender pull, so that she walks evenly toward me and stands there, open and amenable to further direction. Is this what her directors feel? Such power! "Would you mind moving that out of the way?" she asks, at last, gesturing to a plate of brownies. "Sure," I say, smiling, and set my beer bottle down. I've pushed my sunglasses up over my head so my eyes are visible, and she's done the same. We're baring our faces to each other as we move the plates and trays and bowls around, creating space for her covered tray of food. She places her dish on the table and unveils it: stuffed shells, dressed with a light marinara sauce. "Looks delicious," I say, and she smiles. "Did *you* make it?" I ask, not meaning to bear down so hard on the *you*. I feel my face get hot. She lets out a single syllable of laughter and holds my eyes. "No," she says, shaking her head. "Our chef made them—so they'll be edible. More than edible—delicious. If I'd made them, I'd tell you to steer clear." She touches my arm lightly as she says it. This is more than I asked for, more than I even dared to want: her touch! I close my eyes—just for a moment, so as not to seem outrageously weird—and let it fill me.

When I open my eyes again, I notice her smile has slipped a little. The thread between us has gone slack; she's going to walk away. "Does she cook all your meals?" I blurt out. "She cooks most of them, but not all. My husband cooks sometimes," she says. I have her full attention now; the look on her face is one of gentle amusement. The other women on the block ask her things like *What are those beads the baby is wearing?* (A teething necklace.) *Are the girls close?* (Sometimes, but they fight a lot, too.) And so on . . . they try to connect on common maternal ground, but I've approached her like the outsider I am, and she likes it. It's different. Refreshing, even. Her interest in our conversation has thickened—like the glue in one of those mousetraps. She's going to *stay*.

"Does the cook live with you?" I ask, sidling imperceptibly closer to her. I can smell her tasteful perfume. It's delicately spicy, with a touch of musk. She stands with her shapely hands on her hips, opening herself to me, settling in. My arm still tingles where she touched it. "No," she says. "She goes home at six p.m. every day. What about you, are you a good cook?" She's trying to shift the focus to me. Such generosity! I rise to meet it, squaring my shoulders to say, "Yes, sometimes. When I'm in the mood, y'know?" She laughs lightly at this, as if she can't imagine being in the "mood" to cook, because how could she? All she has to do is say, *Jackie, we'll have that scrumptious duck tonight, with the endive salad.* No mood required. "Well," she says, and her gaze shifts over my shoulder, toward the bouncy house, where her girls are still jumping around. "Do you have one of those?" she asks, pointing. "A bouncy house?" I ask, knowing exactly what she means, but going for the laugh. I get it. What a hearty, throaty laugh she has! I know it from her films, of course, but it's an entirely other thing, out here in the wild. I can hardly believe she's unleashed that glorious laugh in response to something *I've* said! "No," she says, recovering. "A kid, do you have a kid?" She's looking at me intently now. *Careful now, careful.* "No," I say. "I don't." I try to say it lightly, breezily, like it doesn't mean a thing, like it isn't weighed down with the agony of years of trying, of my lost marriage, of the terrible emptiness of that extra room, but I fail. Sadness and the bitterness of failure lodge in the back of my throat, and I see that she has seen it. Sensed it. I panic. "But I do have an adorable cat," I say, and she lets that laugh loose once again. This time it has an edge to it, like she's indulging me a little, after my slip, but I don't mind. She sighs then, the kind of sigh you give after having a good laugh with a friend, and then she peers over my shoulder. "It looks like I have to get my girls out of there now," she says. The guy manning the bouncy house is trying, unsuccessfully, to get the kids inside to come out for a new shift of kids waiting in line. "Nice talking to you," she says, touching my arm again, squeezing it lightly as she heads to the bouncy house. I turn and watch her drift away, all silk and goodness and light.

It's exactly what I've wanted, what I've longed for: everything has changed. I float like the actress herself for the rest of the day, smiling at everyone, even at the moms cuddling their babies in those ridiculous front chest packs, even at Mrs. H, even at the strange old man who can't speak but nods and gesticulates when people pass by. I find it impossible to have conversations with anyone else, after talking to the actress, but I get a plate of food with samples from almost all the trays and everything tastes divine: the macaroni and cheese is rich and creamy, the beet salad is satisfyingly tart; the fried chicken is the perfect mix of tender and crisp. It's as if the actress's chef has made *all* the food today. I save her stuffed shells for last. They are *the most* divine: light and fluffy, each bite melts in the mouth. I want to tell her. I want to say, *Your chef has made the most delicious pasta shells I've ever tasted!* But she's caught up in conversations now with the block moms, all that benign and banal chitchat about organic baby food and private preschools. I'm certain she's longing to talk with me again, to that interesting, unusual woman. The special one. The one who surprised her, made her laugh.

I'm standing there feeling peaceful and happily solitary when someone clears his throat behind me. I know that sound. I know that *throat*. I turn with wide eyes to see Nathan there, sardonic smile on his lips, manila envelope in his hand. He looks me up and down for a moment, taking in the dress, and shakes his head, like *tsk tsk*. "Hi there," he says. Like he's just back from his morning jog. *Hi there*. I stare at him some more. "Look, I don't want to make a scene, but you won't answer my calls or texts, or Sandy's calls or texts, so it has to be this way. I had the block party on my calendar and knew you'd be here, so . . ." He's trying to talk in a low voice—I think—but people are starting to glance our way, recognizing Nathan, realizing they haven't seen him for a while, taking in my stricken face. *Do something. You must do something.* It's like someone hissing in my ear. I take a long drink from my bottle of beer, tilting my head all the way back. When the bottle has been drained, I pretend I'm in the classroom, authoritative and calm, but that makes me think of Bernardo. Oh Christ, Bernardo. My face flushes.

Nathan surely thinks it's because of him. *Not everything is about you!* I want to shout. But that would make it even *more* about him than it already is.

"Look, you can't keep being unreasonable," he says tensely. "You have to let me have Cat back. She's *mine.*" "Not anymore," I blurt out. "Really? You're really going to keep playing this game?" he says, his voice rising, his face reddening. The looks from my (once our) neighbors become less surreptitious. One small group inches away from us so they can stare from a safe distance. Suddenly, the actress and her daughters are coming toward us from the bouncy house. I hold her eyes. She smiles, oblivious, and I can see she's about to speak to me. Maybe she'll ask about the shells she brought, or make a joke about me owning a bouncy house. Who knows! She could even say, *We never exchanged names and numbers. You should come over sometime.* That's when Nathan practically screams, "Jesus Christ, pay attention! Can't you listen to me for five fucking seconds?!" The actress's eyes dart from me to him, from him to me. Her smile drops, her face goes blank, and she herds her daughters forward. Past the scary fighting couple. Past the ruined husk of a shared life. "Here," Nathan says. His jaw is tight as he waves the envelope in the air. "These are the papers. The *divorce* papers," he says, still loud, enunciating so that anyone within a twenty-foot radius—which is everyone on our block—can hear. "And if you want to fight over Cat, then be my guest. I thought we could resolve this like two adults, but you're clearly incapable of that. So, I'll see you in court." He slaps the envelope against my chest; I can't help grabbing it before it falls. Nathan, meanwhile, turns and wades through the groups of gawking families and couples and jogs away up the block. Leaving me here. Alone. Surrounded by curious, condescending onlookers. Clutching the envelope against my fine green dress and my strand of dark pearls.

At first there is silence. Frozen, I wait for someone— anyone—to take me by the arm and lead me home, or down the block, or anywhere away from here. But it doesn't happen—there is only that cavernous silence for a few beats, and then the neighborly chatter picks up around me. Slowly it grows to a low hum, surrounding and excluding me, expelling me, even, from its midst. One man laughs at a joke—softly at first, as if he knows it's wrong, but then a moment later his laugh swells into an outright guffaw. He gives in to it, leaning back, his face in the air. I stare at his red face, at the beer in his hand, as he eats the air greedily. He doesn't care. No one cares. No one even bothers to look my way now; now that the show is over, my so-called neighbors are moving on with their block party, on with their lives. What concern is it of theirs, if some lone renter among them has been humiliated and dumped on a city street?

I go on standing there, unable to move, unwilling to flee. If I flee, they all win. Nathan, the neighbors, the lawyers: the lot of them. If I could, I would sink down to the pavement, my skirt billowing around me, and bawl like a baby. The neighborhood children would stream from the bouncy house and circle me, petting my head and shushing me just like their mothers do when they cry. I would stare up at them and smile valiantly through the tears. Instead, here I stand: red-faced and shaken. Not crying. Staring off above the heads of my neighbors, into the blankly reflective third-story window of a nearby brownstone.

I think of the actress, skirting the scene and vanishing into her fantasy house, her fantasy life. At least I saw a touch of empathy on her face—though that could be from years of on-screen practice. But I forgive her. She is the *only* one I forgive. The desire to talk to her, to be in her presence again, wells up so strongly that tears prick my eyes. Lowering my gaze at last, I stare at her front door and will her to come out until . . . her door opens! She walks right out and rejoins the party. A miracle! I can breathe again—in through the nostrils, out through the mouth—and let my arms hang at my sides. The envelope drops from my hand to the pavement. I consider leaving it there for the party-goers to trample with their dirty shoes, but instead I reach down and grab it, march to my building, climb the steps, and shove it through the mail slot. Done. I take a deep breath and survey the scene from the top of my stoop. They're just *people*. Who cares what they saw? What they think? I can handle them and their pitying glances. I'll go back and have more beer and a damn good time and I *will* speak to the actress again. To hell with Nathan and all the rest of them.

The actress is never alone, but I try to stay near her—within ten feet at all times—so I've wound up in myriad pointless conversations with myriad pointless people: namely, the darling neighbors who stood and stared when Nathan humiliated me an hour or so ago. They're doing a great job now, as am I, of pretending that it never happened. The beer helps with this. Between the beer and the warm weather, I feel tipsy and okay with everything—even with the intensely curious looks Mrs. H has been shooting my way since Nathan stormed off. Before I know it, things are winding down. Parents are luring their kids out of the bouncy house and away from the face-painting table. I take some pleasure in watching the inevitable tantrums—the children I've wanted so badly are nothing more than spoiled brats! While I'm watching the family dramas, I spot the actress with Mrs. H. She has a soft spot for Mrs. H, as most people around here do. They see her as our very own grand dame—I'm the only one who thinks she's just a nosy old bitch. I'm watching the two of them nod and talk, watching the actress touch the old lady's arm just as she touched mine. I turn away from the sight and return to the table for yet another beer. Bottle number seven, I think? I've lost track.

Someone comes up behind me. I sense a presence but don't look. Sweating beer bottle in hand, hopes flagrantly raised, I straighten and turn. It's Mrs. H. I must have conjured the old lady with my hateful thoughts. "Are you having a nice time?" she asks with narrowed eyes, like she's waiting for my lie. I nod and smile. Looking over her head, I scan the crowd for the actress. I can't find her anywhere—has she gone? Did she finish talking to the old bag and slip quietly away? Even the beer coursing through my blood can't quell my rising panic. "She's going home," Mrs. H says, so softly that at first I think I've misheard her. "Huh?" I say. "You missed her," Mrs. H says, pursing her lips like she's holding back a smile. "I don't know what you're talking about," I spit out, slurring slightly. She doesn't blink. Doesn't move. I'm the one who has to turn and walk away, which seems unfair. I hear her grunt quietly behind my back. What I wanted to say—to shout—is, *Leave me the fuck alone!* I go stand near the guys deflating the bouncy house—where none of my neighbors are—to cool down. I'm actually staring at my feet when someone says hello near my left ear, and I know at once it's *her*.

"Your salad was delicious," she says, smiling. She's standing there with a wineglass in hand—she must have popped into her house to get it. Mrs. H lied, I see with satisfaction, I *didn't* miss her. I thank her for the compliment and stand there frozen, smiling. I can't think what to say. "Clearly you have no need of a chef," she says, almost shyly. It helps me recover, to see her a little vulnerable and working so hard to be nice. "Oh god, no, I do," I say, rising up at last out of *that* woman to channel my teacher self—the confident professional woman who is heeded, respected, sometimes even adored. "It's the one dish I can do really well, and it's fun to cook for such a big group. I live alone now," I add, inexplicably, before I can stop myself. The actress nods solemnly—of course she knows I live alone, after that scene with Nathan, and now the sad, rejected woman I had handily banished rises before her eyes again. *Idiot!* I would scream, if I could. I had her, I really had her, and now I've just lost her. We stand there smiling awkwardly at each other. Then she gives me a little wave—instead of touching me on the arm, as she did earlier, as she did a moment ago with Mrs. H. "I'm heading in with the girls," she says. "Nice meeting you." But we haven't met, not properly! We haven't even introduced ourselves! She turns and walks away. Leaving me here, dumbfounded and alone, returned to my original, forsaken, despairing, and despised self.

FUCK YOU. When I get home I stare at the last line of Bernardo's latest text. He sent it hours ago, before the block party, and the fact of it sitting there seems to erase the entire day, as if every good and golden moment, along with every shit-smeared one, were swallowed up in a hungry chasm that bears only one message for me: *FUCK YOU*. I'm drunk and disgusted with life, with my fucking a student and fucking up with the actress by exposing her to the garbage of my existence. How could I have tainted even *that*?

*

It hits me sometime later while I sit at my kitchen table, head spinning, taking sips of restorative tea: I know exactly what I have to do to put things right. Not with Bernardo. *Fuck* Bernardo. With renewed energy, I grab my wallet and keys and head to the store. I return with boxes of orzo, one small watermelon, feta cheese, and fresh basil. I walk right past the schmucks who signed up for clean-up duty on the way to and from the store. I don't even bother to wave or shout a neighborly "Thanks!" as they fold and carry chairs, wipe down tables, and pick up paper plates and balled, dirty napkins—all the refuse of the day. It makes me feel dirty just to look at them.

For the first time in months, I feel the purpose and drive I used to have in the kitchen sometimes, whipping up one of Nathan's favorite dishes or trying a challenging new recipe for the two of us. I boil, mix, measure, and taste with something like joy—even as the beer buzz fades, even as Bernardo's message runs like ticker tape across the internal screen of my mind: *FUCK YOU FUCK YOU FUCK YOU*. When I take the first bite of my finished orzo salad, I close my eyes. The internal screen goes blank, and everything, every inch of my being, is engaged in the crisp, summery flavors. It's a victory—it's the *taste* of victory.

I step outside wearing a casual-but-cute bright yellow sundress—one that I bought last year, inspired by *her*—to see all trace of the party gone, though the street remains cordoned off, silent and empty. It gives our block a desolate feel; at either end I see cars and pedestrians passing by, avoiding our block as if something unspeakable recently happened here. I shake off the hollow feeling it gives me and walk confidently down the front stoop like an actor stepping out from the wings of a stage. No neighbors are about, not even Mrs. H, which is just as well, though I like to imagine sets of eyes behind the shuttered and curtained brownstone windows, watching me as I walk down the street, a bright lemon-yellow figure bearing carefully a dish of orzo salad, stepping lightly, easily, breezily, all the way to number 202.

When I stop at the front garden gate, my pulse leaps, beating, to the back of my throat. Should I go to the basement door, as an intimate of the family would? Or up the front stoop to the official door like a servant, a stranger, a Jehovah's Witness peddling her vision of the end? I peer into the basement window, more openly and intently than I've ever had the nerve to do before, at least in the light of day, and see them all there, the actress at the kitchen table holding the baby, the husband leaning on the counter, talking to a staff member, and the two girls busy in the play area. Everyone is there. I feel a little faint—when I'd played the scene in my mind, she alone would come to the door, make a darling O of surprise with her mouth, and then happily take the dish, ushering me in for a glass of wine with a backward nod of her head. *Come in, come join me in my light-filled room.* But this is a different scenario. Shockingly different, though I should have known. It's a Saturday afternoon, post–block party. Of course they're all together. My hands have begun to sweat. I imagine standing here until the dish slips from my hands to crack loudly on the slate tiles of their garden, sending bits of pink and white and green all over—it would be a loud, humiliating signature. She would know exactly who had come to her garden, and she'd shake her head sadly, maybe even angrily, at the sight, before sending a staff member out to clean it all up. No. I can't let this pathetic vision take hold of me. Remember the party! Our warm conversation! Her thrilling touch on my arm! I close my eyes and when I open them, I see someone blur past the window toward the door. I straighten and clear my throat. Walk determinedly to the *basement* door. Just as I balance the loaded dish on one hand and reach for the buzzer with the other, the door behind the basement gate creaks open. A woman dressed in black yoga pants and a bright pink T-shirt, the one I'd seen chatting with the husband a moment ago, is standing there staring at me with a smile on her glossy lips and a frown in her eyes. "Can I help you?" she asks. I smile back. Widely. I see it catch in her eyes—I don't *look* like a dangerous person, I *look* like a beautiful, nicely dressed friend of her employer's, someone who has come for a nosh and a chat. "Hi," I say breezily, "I've come with a dish for the family." The woman cocks her head in what could be a friendly way. She's young and attractive, with her thick black hair pulled back in a sleek ponytail. I wonder what she *does* for the family. Is she one of the nannies? The actress's personal assistant? Their housekeeper? "Oh, how nice," she says, finally moving to open the gate. Relief swells in me and I start to chatter. "She and I spoke about it earlier at the block party—she was a big fan of my dish, so I thought I'd bring her some more. I had extra left from this morning," I add quickly, knowing it would seem too weird to admit to having prepared it just for her. The woman smiles and continues to fumble with the lock. Finally the door swings open and . . . what does she do? She steps toward me, hands out, as if to *take* the dish from me. I shrink back with it against my chest then, shaking my head. "Oh no," I say. "I have to give it to her myself." The suspicious look returns to her eyes, along with a flicker of annoyance, and she steps back from me. "All right," she says. "Let me check with her about it. Where do you live?" she asks, squinting at me. Like it's any of her business, where I live! "Oh, just up the street. We talked at the block party earlier," I tell her again. Heat rises to my cheeks but I try to remember to breathe, calm down and breathe. The woman nods and retreats through the door, closing and locking it behind her—so I won't rush in and kill them all with my dish, I suppose. Ha! While I'm waiting, I try to hold my face in the calmest, friendliest, stillest pose possible. I am calm. I am friendly and sane. I'm your new neighborhood friend, remember? I'm certain *she'll* come out next—after the staff person explains everything to her, she'll smile and say, "Oh, it's okay, I've got this," and she'll step outside to me, her hair and skin and white teeth gleaming in the light, and as she opens the gate she'll laugh and say, *Sorry! My staff can be overprotective sometimes*, and she'll usher me in to join the family gathering. So I wait, my skin prickling with the sensation of coming joy.

While I wait (patiently, so patiently), that unforgettable scene in *Morning's First Light*, one of the actress's first films, comes to mind. She plays an abused young suburban housewife who has an affair with the soon-to-be-doomed pilot who lives next door. It's the scene where the pilot first rings her doorbell late at night. The wife—the actress—comes to the door, while her drunken husband looms threateningly in the shadows behind her. Her green eyes glow bright against the creamy skin of her face, stunning the pilot and all of us sitting in our velvet multiplex chairs. We stare at her in disbelief and something almost like dread—that a creature of such transcendent grace and beauty . . .

The same woman is back—the staff person. She's cleared her throat. "Hi," she says. My heart sinks and my face reddens as she starts to reach for the dish yet again. "I'll take that for you—with thanks from the family!" she says perkily, with a sly smile lighting her face, like this is her entertainment for the day, this strange person showing up at her famous employer's door with a dish of salad. *Pasta salad!* she'll tell her friends, and they'll laugh and shake their heads at the thought of *such a fucking loser.*

I draw the dish back toward my chest involuntarily and stare at her. She draws her own hand back and tilts her head at me, the sly smile now frozen in place. "No," I say firmly. She *won't* laugh at me—no one will. Not her, not the actress, not even the actress's *baby.* "I have to give it to her—to them—directly," I say coldly. I see a flicker of fear in the woman's eyes. She draws back, her hand on the gate in case she needs to slam it quickly, I suppose. "I'm sorry," she says, almost politely. "That can't happen tonight." "Tonight?" I ask sharply. It is not nighttime; this woman is clearly delusional. "I could bring it by another time," I say, careful to keep my voice from shaking. But the woman, the literal gatekeeper, shakes her head. "No, I'm sorry, I'll take it from you now if you like, but there's no other option." Something in me—the socially programmed core of me—starts to relinquish the dish, starts to hand it over as if I were fine with this, as if I'd been planning to do this all along. She reaches her hands out—a little hesitantly, it seems, to take it from me. But five minutes after I've gone, I know she'll chuckle over this whole scene with the family, telling them about the weird things I said, mimicking the expressions on my face and the desperate glint in my eyes. The husband will lean down and sniff the salad; he'll shrug his shoulders as if to say, *I'd eat it.* The actress will roll her eyes. After a gentle nod from her—or maybe an imperial wave of her hand—the staff person will take the dish and dump my delicious, lovingly homemade salad into the trash. The actress, nonplussed, will continue sipping her wine from that infernally elegant glass.

I jerk the dish back—just before the woman's fingers touch it. I turn on my heel and walk right out of the garden. I'm almost certain she's standing there the whole time, watching me go. Fuck *them.* Fuck *her.* Fuck *the actress. FUCK YOU!* I hear a voice scream inside of me—not Bernardo's, mine.

*

When I wake, hours have passed. The apartment windows are dark. It must be nine? Ten? Midnight? I've no idea. I'm slumped by the door in my yellow dress, right where I landed on coming home, shaking with humiliation and rage. I sat there shaking and staring into space, longing for a cigarette but unable to move, and then, somehow, I must have fallen into a dead sleep. The glass dish full of orzo salad sits beside me, still neatly covered in plastic wrap. How could it remain so pristine? After everything that's happened today? I wrap my hands around the edges of the dish and rise creakily to my feet. Every inch of me aches—especially my head. In the kitchen I slam the pasta dish down on the counter, hoping it will break. It does not. I splash water on my face and peer up at the clock. *Three a.m.* Jesus Christ, I've lost *hours* over this wretched day. Over this wretched *salad!* I take the dish and dump all of the pasta into the trash—just as I'd imagined the actress's staff member doing. How funny! If only I could laugh. I grit my teeth and start scrubbing the dish with the rough side of the sponge. I scour the whole thing, front and back, inside and out, in every curved corner, and lay it on the drying rack. It sits there gleaming under the light, so pure, so irreproachable and seemingly inviolable. A moment later, I snatch it from the tray and run to the door. Slide into espadrilles. Run outside and down the steps and down the dark, deserted street to number 202. I pause at the actress's gate for just a moment. The house is dark, and even the outside lights are off. If there's a security camera mounted somewhere, I've never seen it. I take a deep breath and open the gate, pad quietly across the flagstones, and stand in the exact center of their front garden. My hands are sweating where they grip the dish and the giddy feeling in my chest makes it hard to focus but finally I am ready: I close my eyes, raise the dish high, and let go.

It hits the ground with a spectacular crack. Better, and louder, even, than I'd imagined it would be. Panicked, I drop down into a crouch and feel across the slate with my hands. I scoop up several large pieces, crush them to my chest, and run.

Lights must be going on at the actress's house. They must be! As I run home I imagine her, standing groggily at the upstairs window, peering down into the darkness, trying to see who or what it was. *I'll go take a look*, her husband says. The baby has woken from the sound. He starts with small, low sobs that build as the actress stands at the window, transfixed. She shivers, hears his increasingly desperate cries, and goes to him at last, shushing him and holding his head against her breast. She will soothe him with milk, in the rocking chair, and she will not worry about the threatening sound. *Nothing can touch us, not here, not anywhere*, she will tell him. Over and over again, until her head starts to nod in time with the pulse and flow of warm milk.

When I reach my front door, I turn and look down the street. No sign that anyone has woken—no lights have gone on outside or inside the house, as far as I can see. How is that possible? How could they not have been woken by that terrible noise? I stare into the darkness, with my sliced and burning hands still pressing the shards to my chest, feeling my former giddiness fade and shrink to nothing and then—there! The garden light goes on! I've done it! I race upstairs and lock the apartment door behind me. Lean against it, breathing heavily. Laughter bubbles up out of me, shaking me from the inside out. I want to shout, *I'm rich! I'm rich!* Like I've made off with bags of loot instead of the broken pieces of a good glass dish. Somehow, though, I *do* feel rich—absurdly so. I let it fill all the nooks and crannies where my rage once dwelled, let it glow inside and warm me. Then I place the shards carefully in a brown paper shopping bag and set it against the extra room's duct tape wall. Cat has been sitting there expectantly, as if waiting for this offering. Here it is, little one. This is for you.

When I've finally calmed down, I clean my hands at the sink. They sting like hell. I bandage the worst parts and sit down to look at my phone. Bernardo's text is still there. I'm almost surprised to see it. That *FUCK YOU* was not erased by the "fuck you" I just delivered down the block—I thought that it might be, but I find that I don't really care either way.

Cat lies with me all night long, draped over my feet, warming me. I stay in bed until 11 a.m. Wake up still feeling rich, and high. The feeling stays, humming through me, all day long—like new love.

*

There it is, glinting in the sun like an artifact from a lost civilization or an errant god: a sizeable, vaguely triangular glass shard, leaning against the gate at number 202. The rest of the garden has been swept clear, so it can't be a careless oversight. The actress put it there as a sign to me, to say *I know who you are. Stay away from me.* I smart at the imagined words. But maybe I've read this wrong, and the shard says, *I know who you are and I understand your frustration at what happened yesterday. I was wrong. You were right. Let's be friends.* Either way, it's intended for me and I *must* have it. My bandaged fingers itch to grab it. I do a quick pass by her house, stoop gracefully to grab the glass without cutting myself, and keep walking, all the way around the block and back to my own house, in case anyone's watching.

At home I place the shard in the bag with the others. Cat sits beside it, purring contentedly.

*

I have to read the e-mail twice before I understand its meaning:

> Dear Professor:
>   I am writing to inform you that I have contacted your department chair about the inappropriate nature of our

139

relationship. After you expressed displeasure with my academic performance, I felt coerced into having sex with you in order to improve my grade. I have filed a formal complaint with the university's Office of Student Affairs. I have also been withdrawn from your class.

Bernardo

From the top of the mountain, I have been flung down. I lie at the bottom, sick to my stomach. I write only three words to Bernardo: *Are you serious?* He doesn't respond.

Is he bluffing? Is he insane? Has he really done this thing? If he has, my department chair will chuckle to his drunken, slovenly self and then picture the whole scenario as he masturbates in his reclining leather office chair. And then he will fire me—even though I've only done what he himself has done a thousand times, with a thousand young women.

I've heard nothing by the late afternoon, when it's time to head to class. I manage to dress myself with my trembling, injured hands. *Professor T, come back to me*, I think desperately. I can't even conjure her image, though—she's left me for good. And the actress herself? Even she—who can't be the paragon of virtue her onetime character was—even *she* would turn away from me now, pariah-to-be of the English department, creepy female predator of the classroom. I'm left alone to calm myself. If Bernardo is in class, I decide, this has all been merely a cry for attention. I'll soothe him and fuck him and all will be well. But if he isn't there . . . I try not to think about that. On the subway, I stare at the wizened face of a woman across the way until she looks up so abruptly, with such a hard gleam in her eye, that I drop my gaze.

When I first walk into class, I scan the room, looking for him. He isn't there. Everyone else is, though—and staring intently at me. Some of them stare at my bandaged hands, too, but no one asks about them. That would be Bernardo's role, if he were here. I feel terribly shaky for the first five minutes, but as I begin to walk them through Elizabeth Bishop's "One Art," I regain solid ground. I'm fortified by the brisk, blithe tone of the villanelle's refrain: "The art of losing isn't hard to master." My students are fortified by it, too, I can tell—they're fooled by it, in fact. They think, *At last! We're reading a happy poem!* But by the end, when Bishop has walked us firmly to the edge of the abyss, into which her mother, her former homes, and finally, her former beloved have all been unceremoniously tipped, the mood has shifted. Chloe looks as if she's on the verge of tears, and Devon looks angry. Only Simon seems totally unaffected. "Why does she say that?" Joanne asks, frowning. "Say what?" I ask, even though I already know. "That it's easy to lose, that it isn't a disaster, when she clearly doesn't mean it." "Oh," I say softly, "because it's far more powerful to say it this way, isn't it? To say it lightly. It's like a gut-punch. A verbal gut-punch." I'm looking down at the floor as I speak, to hide the tears filling my eyes. I have no idea how Joanne responds, if she responds at all.

*

The next day passes, and the next, without hearing from my department chair. Without hearing from Bernardo. I've become more and more certain that Bernardo was bluffing. Wouldn't I have heard from my chair by now, if he hadn't been? If I don't hear by tomorrow, then I'll know I'm right. At some point Bernardo will send me his blackmail demands and I'll meet them. Whatever they are—more secret rendezvous, an automatic A in the class—I'll grant them, in the name of self-preservation. I can't lose my job or what's left of my life over this ludicrousness.

I'm out for a long walk, glancing sideways at the actress's house as I pass by. I haven't seen her in days. If she saw me, would she shrink back in fear? Or would she look at me blankly, with no sign of recognition? Of the two, her blankness would be worse. It would mean that nothing that has passed between us—not the warm conversation, not the glass dish incident—has meant *anything* to her.

On my way home, I step over the manila envelope Nathan shoved at me on the day of the block party, just as I've done every day since then. But when I reach the stairs today, I pause and turn to retrieve it. Upstairs, I light a match and hold the envelope over the sink to set it on fire. I let the whole thing burn to ash and then wash what's left down the drain. At the end, I pour myself a huge glass of red wine and stand at the window with a cigarette. One gulp of wine, one drag on the cigarette. Repeat. Until the glass is empty and I've smoked the cigarette down to a nub.

The manila envelope has similarly burned down to nothing. Or it was always nothing; it never existed at all.

Maybe it's the act of making one unwanted thing disappear that makes another appear: when I check my e-mail, there's a message from my department chair. Saying nothing, only that he'd like to meet. Just that:

I'd like to meet with you tomorrow. What time are you available?

After the initial, deep stab of fear, I feel something like relief. And calm. It has happened after all—the worst has happened. Which makes me laugh aloud—*the worst?*—the worst happened weeks ago. This is only a minuscule side-bar, an afterthought. I can handle it. I *will* handle it. I will handle my department chair, and Bernardo, and wipe my dirty hands on my jeans and be done.

*

In the morning I wear my black silk blouse with the silver buttons and the deep V-neck. I tuck the shirt into my slim black knee-length skirt with the slight flounce at the bottom. I've put on pantyhose and heels. Silver button earrings and a pendant necklace that hangs like a subtle arrow pointing to the lush cleavage below it. I carry my best briefcaselike black leather bag, and iron my hair to a bright, smooth sheen. I've carefully applied concealer, powder, blush, mascara, and my signature lipstick. I could be stepping out of the door onto a set. I could be stepping beyond that, directly onto a screen. I feel that sense of bright, unassailable performance on the way to the train, while riding the train, and all the way to my chair's office door. I knock briskly. "Come in," he says, clearing his throat. For a moment, my heart flutters like a nervous undergrad's. Then the mask slides into place and I breeze through the door.

"*So* nice to see you, Drew," I begin, smiling as we grip hands. He's smiling, too, and gesturing me to the seat across the desk from him, but I see the quizzical look in his eye. He seems a bit flustered, even. I sit comfortably in the chair and wait, self-assured and still. We chat for a while—lovely weather we're having! Enrollment is down. Computer Science is draining funds from all the humanities departments, it's a damn shame. And so on. Then Drew leans forward, steepling his fingers together like the movie version of a department chair would, and says, "Look, I think you know why I've called you in here." I tilt my head and squint my eyes a bit. I refuse to make this easy for him. He colors and clears his throat. Again. "There's been a complaint against you—from a student in your class. He suggests—no, he *claims*—that there's been a—an inappropriate relationship between the two of you." He sits there, watching me, waiting for a response of some kind. "Oh!" I say, feigning surprise, even touching my hand to the pendant, as if in need of security after such a shock. I watch Drew's eyes flit uncontrollably to my breasts. "But that's ludicrous. I know you can't tell me his name, but I assume it's a student named Bernardo?" I catch his eye and read the silent affirmation there. "I'm not totally surprised, then. He has seemed a bit off since the first week of class, to be honest. I'd almost mentioned it to you, even. Now I wish I had." I am calm at the core of my being. Calm spreads through me from my core to the tips of my fingers and toes. "All the same—" Drew begins, but I hold up a staying hand. "Also, Bernardo's performance in the class has been disappointing—to both of us—so he's clearly cooked this up to try to get an A." I say it coldly, sharply. Drew is staring at me, seemingly at a loss for words. His face is entirely red. It looks like it may stay that way permanently. I hold in the triumphant laugh. Drew seems to be choking or stuttering, trying to get words out. I lean in, like a gentle professional, ready to help soothe him to speak. "He says he has a pair of your panties," he blurts out, at last, and I know instantly that it's true. I remember hastily gathering my clothes while he slept and not finding them. I didn't care at the time—I just wanted to escape. Somehow I manage to roll my eyes. "Really, Drew? I can't believe you'd even dignify that kind of accusation by repeating it." He spreads his hands wide, as if he's innocent, as if he isn't the renowned lecher of the department we all know him to be. As if he hasn't snatched (ha!) his young conquests' panties himself, stuffed them into his coat pocket to sniff and discard before he walks through his own front door, to embrace his wife and pat his children's heads with the very same hand that fingered the panties and what was in them. "Look, I'm obligated to call you in and explain the complaint in detail. It sounds like this is bogus, but if the student presses his case, you'll have to sit in mediation with the dean and work it out. Are you prepared to do that?" He says this all in a rush. I cast my mind back to the underwear I wore to Bernardo's apartment, wondering if it was the distinctive black lacy pair or just one of my regular black cotton ones. It doesn't matter—they won't try to identify me by my underwear, for Christ's sake! And in general it's my word against his, and my word will prevail. I'm a highly regarded female professor, and this student is harassing me! I nod firmly at Drew. "Yes, I'm prepared, though this is a great inconvenience at this busy time of the semester. It seems unfair that I would be put through the ringer for this by some . . . unstable student." Drew nods, seeming to commiserate. He's been there—we all know he's been there. Though his "unstable students" are telling the truth. And so is mine, of course. Drew seems more relaxed, now that all of this is out in the open and I've taken it so well. Remarkably well. I'm one of his best teachers, after all, and a favorite of the students. I would never do something like this—look at me! I'm practically the poster girl for the healthful academic life. Slender, strikingly attractive, fashionably dressed . . . a youthful middle-aged woman who has managed to balance career with home life. He doesn't know about Nathan, of course. No one here does. "How's Nathan?" he asks then, as if reading my mind. It's the first time since the interview began that I lose my cool. My eyes dart to the window behind him, to the view of skyscrapers crowding the horizon and eternal gray sky beyond that. "He's fine," I say absently. I start to gather my things. "Well, I'd like to say I'm happy to have gotten the chance to chat with you, but . . ." I smile, confident again. He matches my smile with his own relieved grin. "Thanks for coming in. I'll keep you updated on any new developments, but I think we've got this one covered." Then he winks at me, he *winks*. I pick up my bag, give him a cheery little wave, and turn to go. "Take care, Drew," I say over my shoulder, and for once I mean it.

I'm practically strutting down the street as I leave the building. Nothing can touch me, not the loud noise of traffic, not the crowds, not even the foul air. I'm as sheltered from it all as the actress would be—or *more* than she would be, because I don't have the prying pairs of eyes, the dropped jaws, the pointing fingers, the tourists sneaking smartphone pics. I'm invisible—except for a few men who, predictably, do double takes as I pass. I ignore them. I feel so light and free I could lift up off the sidewalk and fly all the way home.

I'm just climbing the steps of my stoop when the guy who'd been walking nonchalantly toward me says my full name and I turn. He shoves a manila envelope into my hands (another goddamn manila envelope—a chill rides my spine at the sight—as if the first one has been resurrected from the ashes) and says, "Cheers. You've been served." Then he spins away from me, down the street.

It's a subpoena. To appear for a mediation with Nathan on December 3. Fucking Nathan. Topics to be covered: *Custody of Cat* appears first and foremost on the page, amid a garble of legal language I can barely focus on through the shaking veil of my rage. *Custody of Cat. Custody of Cat.* I close my eyes, standing there on the stoop, and imagine ripping Nathan's head off, literally *ripping it off*, and tossing it here in the corner of our little front garden. I'd leave it there for the rats to eat. They'd eat his eyes first, I suppose, and then the soft curve of his nostrils. Or maybe they would start with his plush lips. I think I could even stand to watch them do it. I think I would even *applaud* as they did it, until they'd stripped off all the flesh and hair and loveliness of his face and left nothing but bone. The motherfucking bone of Nathan.

I run up the stairs, two at a time, and when I get into the apartment I throw the envelope on the floor and scream, "Cat!" over and over again. She doesn't appear. I remember myself, lower my voice, call to her in a gentle tone, cluck my tongue the way I do when her food is ready and waiting for her in the kitchen. At once she comes padding toward me, mewing. I scoop her up and press my face into her soft fur. I start to grip her too tightly, perhaps, because she struggles in my arms. When I finally release her, she lands on all four paws (of course! perfect creature!), and pads into the kitchen to check her bowl. *My* cat. Mine.

*

A deep stillness comes to my life then, as if everything were buried under snow, and I the lone figure moving through the hushed landscape. I imagine the actress in a movie like this, maybe one about survival in the wilderness, or after an apocalypse. How brave and ruggedly beautiful she would be, stripped of all excess—no makeup, jewelry, or fancy clothes—becoming one with nature, killing squirrels or fish and biting into them raw, leaving the blood smeared on her face as the camera zoomed in to show us her bright eyes and stoic chewing. How magnificent she would be!

Meanwhile I keep moving along my well-worn track, unmagnificent and mostly invisible—except when I'm teaching. I go to class and back home, to the store and back home, for a walk and back home, and every time I stop in front of the actress's house; I see signs of life through the kitchen window—various combinations of the husband, the children, and the staff—but never *her*. I eat. Drink.

Sleep. Repeat. There has been no word from Drew about Bernardo, no word from Bernardo, no word from Nathan about the pending mediation. I never wrote it down in my calendar, but I can't seem to forget the date, no matter how hard I try: December 3. If only the actress could take my place on *that* day. She would dress in a smartly fitted black suit, augmented with tasteful jewelry and low black heels. Everything about her would be calm and grave and graceful. Nathan's lawyer would look at him in disbelief, as if to say, *You want to take something from* her? The whole thing would turn quickly in her favor. She would leave with the rights to Cat's ownership tucked firmly beneath her slender, suited arm. A slight smile on her face—part victory, part grief-shadow—having won but having put to rest, forever, her relationship with Nathan. *My* relationship with Nathan. How much tidier it would be if she could do that for me.

*

This morning I wake to a crisp chill in the air, the start of weather that used to bring me such joy. I always looked forward to making soups and stews, and to cuddling with Nathan on the couch and watching one of our Netflix shows. No more! I have only Cat to cuddle with now—I try to satisfy myself with that, with her solid warmth and purring softness, but December 3 looms too large in my mind. Though it's still weeks away, the day hangs over me like a swinging ax. One wrong move and *pfft*—it's my head, not Nathan's. The sound of it swinging above me makes it impossible to relax into my cozy autumn togetherness with Cat. I go through the motions—curling up, eating soup, watching TV—but there is always that infernal sound.

*

I come home one night after class, having squelched Joanne's annoying concern over Bernardo's disappearance with a vague statement about "personal issues," and collect the mail from the front hall. I see a formal-looking letter from the university and feel the first flutter of panic. Will I have to sit in mediation with Bernardo after all? Or is it just my spring teaching schedule? I tear open the envelope. Inside is a letter from Dean Polaski, a woman I've met only a handful of times over sushi rolls and wine at official department functions. After a suspiciously warm opening, she writes:

> As you know, enrollment in our humanities departments has been steadily shrinking since the fall of 2014. The causes are many and varied, and I am certain you've noticed the decreasing number of students in literature classes in particular. Unfortunately, due to this and other

factors, we cannot renew your contract as Lecturer after this coming May. You will complete this academic year's courses as planned, but unfortunately we will not be able to welcome you back in the fall.

Please direct any questions you may have about this matter to my office or directly to your chair. We thank you for your excellent service in the past and wish you the very best in your future endeavors.

Sincerely,

Linda Polaski

Dean, Humanities Division

The first thing I do is dial the chair's number. It rings and rings. I'm certain he sees my name and doesn't pick up. When I hear his happy, boozy, bastardly voice on the message, I wait for the beep and scream, "You goddamn hypocritical son of a bitch!" Then I sit there, letting the silence drag and bloom until the system shuts me off.

Next I sit calmly down at my computer and send a message to my class—deleting Bernardo's e-mail address first—with the subject heading: NEXT CLASS: CANCELLED. In the body, I write:

Dear class, due to circumstances beyond my control, I must cancel our next class. Please keep up with the assigned readings (check the syllabus), and begin work on your final paper. I hope to see you next week.

"Hope" leaves it open, of course, for a further cancellation, which may follow this one. The dean and my chair would be appalled if they knew I had cancelled two classes already, but: screw them. They've already so viciously screwed me.

I lean back against my desk chair and let the panic swell. It pulses at my temples. It brings my recently eaten lunch to the back of my throat. What in god's name will I do, in this insanely expensive city, without a job, without a partner to pick up the slack? How will I live? I force myself up out of the chair and put on my tennis shoes.

At some point I notice that night has fallen. I have no idea what time it is, though—I've left my phone at home. I think I've remembered to bring my keys, but I can't be sure. I can't feel them on my body anywhere, and I have no strength to check—all I can do is walk, arms hanging listlessly at my sides, and look. Parents shepherd back-packed children home from school. Dog shit sits piled in a tidy pyramid by a fire hydrant. Red lights turn green and then yellow. Cars move through the streets, drivers forever honking. At the least provocation, they honk. The noise comes to me muffled, as if it were underwater—or as if I were. My feet ache. I need water. I don't care. Eventually I turn, though, and head back toward my own corner of the neighborhood. It takes a long, long time, but at last my feet carry me exactly where I expect them to go: not home, no, but to the front gate of the actress's house. Where they stop. I lift my eyes.

Finally, our schedules have aligned. The actress is at home, and plainly visible. It's a gift, and one I sorely needed after today's hellish surprise. I see her standing by the back table, bending over her seated eldest girl, who must be doing homework. The actress is giving her advice, or encouraging her, or chastising her gently. Meanwhile the cook is busily preparing dinner at the stove, managing two steaming pots and a sizzling pan at once. When the husband enters the room, possibly after a long day, he greets his wife with a kiss on the lips, and his daughter with a kiss on her duly bent head. He stands with the two of them, chatting. Telling the actress about his day. Asking about hers. Connecting. Listening. For a moment I feel like I belong in this familial triangle, like I'm part of the shape that makes them whole and wholly beautiful. I feel reverent and warm. No longer cast out, no longer dejected or forsaken. No longer the stranger banging on their basement door: *Let me in.* I, too, am cherished and kept. Free from the struggle of daily living. Held gently in my stately home by the gleaming wood floors and the tastefully painted walls and the husband and the children and all of the stainless steel appliances and the delicious meals made by the cook.

I come back to my body with a jolt. I stumble away from the cozy domestic scene and make it back, somehow, to my building's entry hall before I start to wail. Sobs break out of me, knocking the breath from my chest. I grab the banister and drag my feet up the stairs, though it wouldn't matter if I stayed in the downstairs hall wailing because no one is there to hear me, in the empty rooms. Emptiness inside, emptiness outside: this is what's mine. I hold on to the railing outside my apartment door and just let the sobs come buckling out, let them usher the fear and despair out of my body. This is not my life! This cannot be my life! I never thought it would be. I envisioned a sunlit, stylishly decorated place, with books lining the shelves and a beloved's arm holding me. I envisioned children playing in the backyard as I smilingly went about menial household tasks. I envisioned myself as a tenured academic, wrapped safe in the belly of an institution for all time. I envisioned myself as a good woman, a great woman—the best! Better than the actress, happier than the actress, more alive and connected to life than the actress could ever hope to be, trapped as she is in the velvet prison of fame. I would have been free, held only within the soothing bonds of family and home.

But here I am, back in my lonesome, loathsome reality. I finally open my apartment door and step into the small, dark place I call home. All I can hear is the grating sound of Cat's desperate meow, saying, *Too late, too late. Everything you've wanted has slipped away.* Cat curls herself around my legs, mewing and mewing, and all I can think is *shut up.* I scoop her up in one hand and cover her mouth and nose with the other but she squirms and bites my middle finger, so I drop her. She skitters away. After a moment's pause, I go after her, find her crouched beneath the kitchen table. I grab her up, take her to the bedroom, and stuff her under what was Nathan's pillow. Her back legs thump and scratch against my arms, drawing blood, as I press down. "No!" I cry out. But there is no one to hear me.

Finally there is silence and stillness in the dark bedroom. I, too, am still. Tears track steadily down my cheeks, but inside is only a heavy, dead calm.

It was an accident, I plan to tell Nathan. She fell from one of our windows left open by the super after he fixed something or she gobbled up a string that twisted around her insides—I don't know. She died. She simply died. They sometimes do, cats. It's not like there would be an autopsy, or a trial, for the death of a cat. I bathe the scratches all along my wrists—savoring the sting of the soapy water—and bandage them up as best I can.

Oh, Cat! For the second time today I'm on my knees, letting the sobs rack and ravage me. How could I do what I have just done? And why? What good has it done me? I kneel on the carpet, staring at my hands through the blur of tears. My empty hands! I have emptied them myself! I clench my hands into fists and pound them into my stomach. Again. Again.

*

Hours later. Early morning light fills the windows. When I've dressed, I wrap Cat's soft, stiffening body in the old blanket she loved to lie on. I take her downstairs and dig a tiny grave for her with the snow shovel in the front garden. The dirt is packed hard, so it takes a while. I'm sweating and light-headed after the first few shovelfuls. People walk by as I work—curious, appalled, or concerned, I imagine. I feel their eyes on my back—I feel their interest lift me up. Who knows, the actress herself could be walking by. I dig harder, faster. When I'm finally done, I feel a strange satisfaction standing over the grave, breathing heavily and wiping my brow. Like I've earned her death, or atoned for it. I set her body in the hole and cover it with earth. There is a small mound over Cat's body. Hardly noticeable. I smooth it down with my bare hands and close my eyes. *Dear precious Cat, always mine, forever mine, forgive me,* is the silent prayer I make. I imagine how peaceful the scene would be to a passerby: woman kneeling in her dirt-streaked clothes at the foot of a minuscule grave, solemn and prayerful and dignified.

I shower thoroughly, shampooing and conditioning my hair, following the directions on the bottles down to the last line. I clean and scour every crevice of my body: elbows, armpits, butt, vagina. Nothing will stink or be sour once I'm done. Nothing will soil my clean resolve. Cat is gone, I have smothered and buried and mourned her. I am profoundly sad but also proud of my resolve. What it took to kill her! How strong and ruthless I had to be! These are skills—qualities—that can help me carry on with the rest of what I must do to set things right.

Still wrapped in a towel after my shower, I tear down the tape wall leading to the extra room. There's no need for it now, without Cat to worry me. I had almost forgotten that she was the reason I'd needed it in the first place. The wall feels ancient, like it's been in place since before we moved in. But of course it hasn't, and now I want to be able to see and touch all the precious objects I've gathered. I'm tearing down the tape at a feverish pace when the bright pink paint of the actress's daughter's bike catches my eye. I haven't seen it since I brought it in, but there it is, still shining beautifully in the dark. As if it were propped in the store, waiting for someone to buy it. When the tape has all been stripped away, I stand in the doorway and turn on the light, staring around at the tidy piles of things. Then I move among them, touching random objects, crouching down now and then to examine something. There are things I haven't thought of in months, or even years, layering the floor, desk, and shelves. Pristine sets of children's books, faded but hardly worn sweaters, expensive-looking girls' shoes, a frankly hideous straw hat with a red-and-gold-plaid ribbon around it, glue sticks, pots of glitter, tiny bottles of nail polish, a portable radio, and a small bucket of hair accessories, perfect for a young girl. All of this treasure is mine—even the pile of broken shards that I myself created. I sit down in the center of the room, surrounded by my trophies, breathing in the atmosphere of satisfying fullness.

But as the minutes tick by, something shifts. Imperceptibly at first, then it weighs on me heavily: all of this *stuff*. It carries too much of my history. It bears witness to what I've done, who I've been, how I've been wronged and abandoned and lost and emptied out and wronged again. How I've raged, how I've *killed*. I get up and walk from the room and wish I had never taken the tape wall down. My eyes are tearing, and my skin is itching all over. *Close it up!*

I put up a new tape wall, strip by strip, as quickly as I can. For an hour or so, I manage to sit calmly on the couch with a glass of wine, feeling liberated, light and free. Then the heaviness creeps back—the weight of all those things. How can I go on living with them? I feel them watching me through the wall—as if they had eyes! All the same, this must be what the actress feels like—eyes always on her, penetrating her secret corners, unearthing her innermost desires and fears, every waking moment of her life. A wave of pity and grief washes over me—for her, for me, for *us*.

It hits me like a revelation. I want to *show* her that I understand, that I know now how it feels. I want to share this with her, too. And it dawns on me that I *can*.

For the second time tonight, I take the tape wall down.

*

I stand in her front garden with the first box in my hands. It is almost 3 a.m. I'm dressed in black, like last time, but I will perform my duties in silence this time. There will be no furious crash—she will see how I have moved through recklessness and anger to an artful understanding and solidarity. She will have no choice but to see it!

It takes eleven trips total. I've long since sweated through my black clothes. I'm out of breath and feel light-headed every time I climb the stairs, but I'm also determined to stay focused, to do things *right*. Everything looks very tidy and interesting when I'm done—like an installation. The boxes are neatly stacked, one on top of another, and the bicycle is out in front of all of them, gleaming in the faint moonlight. I've draped some clothes along the gate in a festive way—a beige cardigan here, a light pink turtleneck sweater there. I've removed all the children's shoes from their boxes and lined them up neatly along the front fence, in order of size. It's like watching the actress's children grow up before my eyes, scanning from the tiny balletlike slippers to the larger bejeweled sneakers, and finally to the almost adult-size green rain boots. When the actress wakes, she will see this whole tableau I've created for her—this whole tribute to her life as a mother, actress, and wife. As a *human being*. It's my way of saying, *I see you. But also, I know how hard it is to be seen!* As a final touch, I carefully place the shards that were once my glass dish in the seat of a child-size foam armchair, which is itself balanced on top of two boxes. It looks like the final tier of a towering wedding cake, the crown on my visual masterpiece. My loving, original homage.

It dawns on me as I stand there admiring the scene: What if someone comes by and takes something before the actress wakes? If even one small thing were removed from the display—a pair of shoes, a windbreaker, that glistening bike!—it would ruin the order and balance of *everything*. I steal back to my building and sit on the top step of the stoop, staring toward her house, shivering slightly and smoking one cigarette after another.

Four a.m., or thereabouts. I've drifted off a few times, but always snap back awake before too long. There have been only a few stragglers in the last hour—one group of very drunk guys, arguing loudly about a soccer game, who passed right by without noticing it. One homeless man staggered by later, with a rotten bag slung over his shoulder. He glanced at the actress's house, and paused slightly—every muscle in my body tensed—but ultimately he shook his head and moved on. But right now, a figure I instantly recognize is coming up the block. She's a homeless woman I've seen around here for years, a prematurely aged white lady with dark glasses and a rat's nest for hair. She always wears the same shapeless, ankle-length denim dress, tied loosely at the waist, and she pushes a grocery cart full of her junk to and fro. Here she comes, and I know, I just *know* she's going to notice the actress's house. Indeed she does. She pauses, looks around as if looking for a camera—or for me!—and then bends down to inspect the shoes. All at once, I find myself racing down the steps, then the sidewalk, at full speed. Before I've even gotten close, she looks up, startled, wheels her cart around, and takes off running herself. I stand huffing in front of number 202, hands on my hips, surveying any possible damage. She didn't touch a thing. Well, she touched a thing but didn't *take* it. Thank god.

I go back to my house and resume my post. The minutes and hours tick by, the neighborhood wakes, people walk their dogs, others go briskly off to work, heels tap tap tapping on the slate. Nothing moves at the actress's house. Then it happens. The basement gate swings open. The youngest girl runs out, then stops in her tracks. The older girl steps out behind her, and also freezes. Then, at last, the actress emerges. Her eyes widen, her mouth hangs open. She pulls the girls to her. Clutches them. Ushers them through the garden to the sidewalk, still staring, still looking terribly afraid. She pulls out her phone and dials someone, speaks rapidly while looking back at the house. It is not exactly the reaction I wanted, but nevertheless it thrills me. Deep in my gut. It's a deeper feeling, even, than when I stood and chatted with her at the block party that day and she touched my arm—twice. I savor the moment—too long. By the time I stand up, realizing I need to run inside, I'm caught, helplessly staring as they pass. When the actress looks up, she recognizes me, I'm sure of it this time. She *knows* me, of course she does! I hold up a hand—to wave or to stop her from leaving, I'm not sure which—but she doesn't pause. She speeds up, hustling her daughters up the street to school. I've never seen her look as disheveled as she does today; her hair needs combing and her tired eyes want liner or mascara. Her lips could use some Divine Wine. She looks like I usually do when I'm trudging to or from the grocery store. I feel lonely when she goes, but also satisfied. I've done a good day's work. An important, difficult, *necessary* day's work. Even the habitual ache of loneliness can't undo that.

Later in the morning, when the urge to see the entirety of what I made for her takes me by the throat, I put on some sweatpants and a T-shirt (out for a jog—ha!) and head down the block. I can see movement in her front garden. My heart speeds up. I quicken my pace. When I get there, I see several staff members carrying boxes into the house. One of them is *that* woman, the one who barred the door after the block party, the one who caused the incident with the dish. When I get close enough, she happens to look up from her labors—I see that she's pawing through one of the boxes, and after working so hard to collect these treasures it pains me, literally pains me, to see *her* touching them!—and when she sees me, she freezes. As I move along, I feel her eyes burning into my back, accusing me, hating me—for something that has nothing to do with her! What does she know about any of this? Nothing. Nothing at all.

At home I head right for the closet to get out my cleaning supplies. First I vacuum the extra room thoroughly, and then I dust and polish the furniture, the window ledges, the windows themselves, and in some places, the walls, where things had been stacked against them, leaving marks. When I'm done, the place is clean and stark. Beautiful. It looks almost like it did when we first moved in: fresh and promising, a place where I can reinvent my life. I sit down on the area rug in the room and breathe deeply. The lemony smell of the cleaning solutions revives me—after Nathan left I threw out all of his worthless organic cleaners and replaced them with Clorox, 409, Windex, and Pledge. And look at this spotless room! That herbal crap couldn't have done such a thorough job. One more way in which Nathan is dead wrong. And dead *to me*. Ha!

In this moment of satisfaction and high confidence, I get out my phone. Text Nathan: *Cat died last night. Signing divorce papers now.* After I shower—wrists still stinging under the hot spray—and dress for the day, I sit directly down at my desk and sign the divorce papers, fold them neatly, and insert them into the stamped envelope so thoughtfully provided by Platz, Hodder, and Wright. I resist the urge to write *GOOD RIDDANCE* in black marker on the back of the envelope. Then I sit at my computer and begin to work on my CV and cover letter. I will begin a job search today. I will find something suitable, convenient, and *better* than the job I've had for so many years. I'd felt stagnant there for ages, truth be told. This will be the start of a whole new life for me: Nathan is purged from my life forever, the mess with Bernardo is finished, I have no children weighing me down, Cat is gone, and I have shed my dead old job as well. As for the actress, I've laid my cards on the table—or her belongings on the stoop, I should say. New beginnings! I feel more alert and alive than I have in weeks, and I have my own initiative to thank for it. I should have taken charge like this ages ago.

Later in the day, after hours spent searching the academic job listings on the MLA website and updating my CV, I stand in the empty extra room to inhale those scents again, get a hit of renewed purpose. The chemicals have faded, though, since I've left the window open to air them out, and in the late afternoon light the room looks more sad and empty than refreshingly stark, the old dresser still scarred beneath its recent polish, the walls a dingy off-white, with streaks of brightness where I've wiped them. It looks as ragged as I've come to feel, and as empty as my womb has always been.

And Cat. I miss Cat. How she would curl her tail around my legs and purr until I picked her up. How she could fill my arms and a room with her warmth and soft noise. My eyes start to tear but I wipe at them angrily, gritting my teeth. Such nonsense.

I leave to mail the envelope, and return with a new roll of duct tape. Once again, I put the tape wall back up, piece by piece, until the doorway is completely covered.

I go outside for a walk. Instead of pacing the streets as I usually do, I head for the park, recalling my now-distant fantasies of fucking the actress's husband with an almost painful mix of pleasure and guilt. The park is full of winding little paths, mostly used by drug dealers during the weekday afternoons, but I brave them anyway—what could they possibly do to me? Rape? Murder? Sell me pot (the most likely)? I'm not afraid. When I reach the gazebo, it's occupied by a human-shaped lump—or two of them?—moving under blankets. Whatever's going on in there is sickening. Unclean. I quickly turn around, head back up the path.

When I get home, my phone is lit up with texts. Nathan, I'm sure, but I don't check. Instead, I stand at the tape wall and press my face against it. It feels cool and slick against my skin, but I can sense the awful weightlessness of the room behind it. I try to recapture what I felt right after I cleaned it, that sense of pure accomplishment. Now I stand here feeling nothing but empty empty empty and I press my face harder into the tape to try to stop the tears but they come anyway, faster and faster until I have to sink down onto the couch and just let them come. When the sobs finally subside, I can't help myself. I reach for the phone and see just what I expected to see: hatred and ugliness from my ex.

What the hell have you done to Cat? She was perfectly healthy—I know she didn't just die. You're sick. You're really sick. I don't even believe you that she's dead. But if she IS, I know YOU did something to her. And that's incredibly fucked up.

What the fuck is wrong with you??

It's hard to read, but I do, several times over, letting the words sink in one lacerating letter at a time. I stare at my phone screen for an hour at least, long enough for the words to lose all meaning, for the letters themselves to reduce down to strange symbols from an alien tongue. The windows darken. It's time to open a bottle of wine.

*

The extra room nags at me. I shouldn't have emptied it out! I should have just taken everything out of the boxes and decorated the room with my spoils—it would have kept me connected to her, and prevented this sickening hollowness. But all of it is gone—all of the things I worked so hard to accumulate, all of my *treasure on this earth*. I want to tear down the tape wall and reclaim what I relinquished and feel my life full again.

Too late, too late, little fool, Cat would say, in her small, ghostly voice.

Lying on the rug in my living room, staring up at the cobwebbed ceiling fan, letting my mind drift, an image begins to form.

A very strange image.

It's the actress, sitting cross-legged in my spare room—the baby's room, the extra room—trapped there, held there, *living* there. Wouldn't she breathe a sigh of relief at finally being unseen, safe within walls, in my company only? All of the onerous duties and complexities of her life would drop away. We would have such talks! Over wine or tea; over light, delicious meals or sumptuous candlelit dinners. Whatever she needed or wanted, I would provide for her. The scenes of our imagined life fill my stomach with a warmth that surpasses what I feel from the almost-full bottle of wine I've drunk. Surpasses, even, what I felt for the belongings of hers I used to have, and for Cat, and for the husband I used to have, too. What is he now, after all? Only a cold, hard lump in the pit of my stomach. Meaningless.

If I were to do it, to make it real, I would start simply. I'd monitor the actress's comings and goings—like I already do, but with more rigor. I'd watch her jog by in spandex toward the park at 6 a.m., and jog back home forty-five minutes later, her skin glowing with sweat. She'd walk the girls to school a bit later, an arm draped over each one's shoulder as they meandered up the block. I would do my best to be invisible. I could even watch from inside my building's front door sometimes to keep her or anyone else from becoming suspicious. Once I'd mapped out her schedule, I would choose the easiest time to get her alone— probably the early morning jog—and then I'd wait for the right moment.

A kitchen knife and a quiet threat should nicely do the trick. Though I would hate to start things off that way.

In the meantime, I'd ready her room—the spare room, of course. I'd order a futon, pillows and sheets, an easy chair and reading lamp. I'd set it all up to be cozy and soothing—a safe little nest. I'd need to install a door, and I suppose I'd have to have the locksmith return and install a dead bolt on it—and pay him extra to keep quiet, too.

What about the window? I'd want her to have the view—she deserves a view!—but I couldn't risk having anyone see her. Couldn't risk her signaling for help, or even leaping out to escape. It's a shame, but it would probably be best to board up the window. I'd cover it with a lovely curtain, of course. And take her out periodically—to the living room, I mean—for supervised window time.

Her screams would not be a problem. There's no one below us to hear.

When the day finally came, I would bring my sharpest kitchen knife, a Christmas gift from Nathan's mother, and I'd come up behind the actress and grip her shoulder, pressing the knifepoint to her back so she'd gasp just a little. "Don't scream, don't do anything," I'd say. "You'll be fine.

Follow me." And she'd let me push her up the block, up my stoop, up to my apartment.

"You on break already?" A voice—Mrs. H's—intrudes before I can get the actress safely to the spare room. I find myself sitting on the front stoop, wineglass in one hand and cigarette, with long, drooping ash, in the other. "Huh?" I say, confused and still caught up in the dream. "You on break? You going somewhere? Or you just going to sit on that stoop all day?" She grins at this, showing her rotted teeth, or what I suppose are her rotted teeth. I grin back, showing my pearly whites. We're like two fiercely grinning gorillas facing off. "For now I'm going to sit here, yes. Nice seeing you, Mrs. H," I say, using Nathan's technique. She drops her grin and grunts a little in response. I'm fuming helplessly because she has punctured the skin of my fantasy and it's gone now. I can't get it back. She starts to wander off to her own stoop, but she stops abruptly and turns to me, holding on to the fence for balance. "You know they're moving, don't you?" she says. A line of sweat sprouts at my hairline. "Who?" I ask, my voice higher than I want it to be. She doesn't answer, but her eyes soften as if she's sorry for me. I try to keep my own eyes steady on hers even though I'm shaking—my hands are shaking. My lips are trembling. My heart is stuttering. "No," is all I can say. She stares at me for a long minute, then shrugs. "Suit yourself," she says, turning to hobble off at last.

It's not true. It can't be true. She wouldn't *leave*. This is her *home*. Mrs. H must have heard wrong. She might even have made it up just to torment me. Just to watch the cloud of fear pass over my face. Sick.

Over the next few days, I stalk the actress as if I were planning to carry out my fantasy plan after all. I walk by her house or sit on the stoop or stand behind my building's front door and monitor her comings and goings so I can ascertain that Mrs. H was dead wrong, the actress *isn't* moving. Each day that I watch her, I feel better—stronger, steadier. Yesterday she walked home with shoulder bags full of vegetables, fruit, and flowers, from what I could tell—a solo trip to the farmer's market. Today she works alongside her staff members in the garden, readying the greenery for winter. Lifting a small evergreen into the ceramic tub that sits on the top step of their stoop, smoothing the soil around its base. She does it tenderly, lovingly. Would she take such care with a plant she was planning to leave? She isn't moving and she probably never will! Mrs. H, as usual, was delusional and meddling. If only *she* would move.

*

One morning, after the actress's jog but before she takes the girls to school, I walk by her house. I'm no longer worried about her leaving the block, but I've kept watching her anyway. It's been helpful to have a new routine, a new purpose.

As soon as I approach the house, I see it: the sign. In her front garden. A very discreet sign that nonetheless says FOR SALE in bold black-and-white lettering. FOR SALE. It says other things too—the name of the Realtor, the contact number, the blah blah blah blah blah blah blah—but all I see is FOR SALE. A rushing noise fills my head and suddenly I can't breathe. I grasp the top of her fence and stand there gasping, staring at the signpost—not at the sign—at the post where it enters the dirt of their small garden, where it *pierces* the dirt, killing whatever nascent plants might be struggling to break free and find air. *HOW COULD THEY DO THIS? HOW COULD SHE DO THIS TO ME?*

*

Nine a.m. I'm at home drinking wine. I was *guzzling* it, but now my pace has slowed. The glass shakes in my shaking hand. The actress is leaving. The actress is leaving. No—the actress is *trying* to leave. She *cannot* leave. I cannot let her.

I have to talk to her. Talk sense into her. Isn't that what the actress herself would do, in one of her roles? As the street-smart detective, the no-nonsense hooker, the firm and protective young mother?

I spend the rest of the day on the couch, watching the movies of hers I own or can rent. *Dangerous Game* has just been released for rental on Amazon. *Finely Tuned* is streaming on Netflix. I have DVDs of *The Sultan of Hanover Street, Slow Tremor, Morning's First Light, Working Class,* and even *Black Wave,* that blockbuster that announced her official arrival on the Hollywood scene and enabled her to buy her house *on this block. Where she belongs.* I drink these movies in with my wine and eat only popcorn all day and lie awake for hours practicing my lines.

I dream that she's with me in the spare room, but the room as it used to be—full of her discarded belongings. She's going through each box with me, lifting each item and explaining its origin and use, as well as the feelings and memories she attaches to it. She is patient and kind, and happy to be sharing her life with me. We laugh often. Her eyes tear up at the sight of a tiny onesie her daughter once wore. *She wore this in the hospital as a newborn,* she tells me. *She was premature and had to stay in the NICU for weeks.* The tears roll steadily down her cheeks now and she holds up the tiny matching hat the baby wore. *I thought she was going to die*, she says. *I thought I would lose her and then I'd die myself. Those weeks were the worst of my life*. I tell her I understand. And I do. Somehow, I do. I'm crying, too, and we stand there, watching each other weep in complete silence and companionship until morning comes and I wake in bed alone, with a cold and damp face.

*

Six a.m. Like clockwork, the actress comes running down the block. She will pass my house on the way back to hers. When she gets close enough, I clear my throat quietly and rise from where I've been sitting on the stoop. I've dressed in exercise clothes, too, though of course I haven't exercised in days. I hardly moved all day yesterday! Still, it makes me feel more assured, matching her this way. As she gets closer, she doesn't make eye contact, doesn't look up or wave or make any acknowledgment of my presence, but I stand up and hold my hand in the air. "Wait!" I say, though this is not what I'd planned to say. Her head turns slightly in my direction and then I'm amazed to see her picking up speed, running now toward her house as if she were being chased, as if I really were holding the kitchen knife in my hand. "Wait!" I say again, louder, more urgently this time, and I get up and take off after her, running faster than I expected. She's ahead of me but so close I can see the sweaty, freckled back of her neck, see the slight muscles in her biceps bulge as she pumps her arms, hear her breath come in hard, short bursts. I'm nearly close enough to touch her when she yells, "Help! Help!" and turns into her open garden gate and slams it behind her, but I push it open and catch her on the second stair of the stoop, I catch her arm, I touch her where she touched me at the block party, and as she struggles to pull away from me I manage to get out, "We . . . have to . . . talk," while gasping for air. She tugs her arm free and races up the steps, fumbles for her keys, saying, "Shit, shit," the whole time, until she finds the right key and twists it in the lock. I'm down on the second step, panting, watching her from below like we're in one of her movies, like she's about to escape the would-be killer or the enraged ex-lover. But when she runs into the house and slams the glass-paned front door behind her, it jolts me out of my reverie. She locks the door as I walk deliberately to the top of the stoop. We stand there looking at each other; I'm calm now, but she's red-faced, wild-eyed. I notice, suddenly, that she's holding her phone to her ear, talking to someone. Who has she called? The police? Before I know it, I'm pounding on the glass door with my fists, screaming, "What are you doing! What are you doing!"

When I feel a gentle touch on my back—like a lover's touch, or a child's—for one irrational moment I think, *It's the actress.* Even as I watch her talking heatedly into the phone I think, *It must be the actress.* But when I whip around it isn't her, of course—it's Mrs. H—who tried to tell me, who was right all along, who must be gloating now, seeing me crazed at the actress's door. "Calm down," she says softly, her face close to mine, her hands gripping my shoulders. "You have to calm down, you're going to get yourself in big trouble." She doesn't sound like she's gloating; she sounds gentle and chiding—almost as if she were talking herself, not me, out of acting this way. She's so caught up that there are *tears* in her eyes. Anger rises up in me hard and swift, and I shove my hands into her chest. "Not you!" I scream. Her gray eyes go wide. She teeters, then stumbles and starts to fall. The glass door bursts open and I hear the actress say, "Peggy!" When I turn, she's reaching her arms out—not to me, but to Mrs. H. But it's too late. The old lady falls backward down the ten brownstone steps, her arms spinning helplessly. Her head hits the sidewalk with a sickening thud. "Peggyyyyyy!" the actress screams, hysterical now. We stand motionless, side by side at the top of the steps. Sirens sound in the distance. The actress is the first to move. She runs down the steps to Mrs. H—to *Peggy.* I watch her touch the body lovingly, carefully, and pull it onto her lap to cradle the battered head against her chest. I think of last night's dream, of the story the actress told me about her newborn daughter, and I wonder if it's true.

She looks so comfortable in this pose, as if she's used to it, the posture of loss. It's beautiful—stunning, even—and despite everything I feel myself relax. As if I were seated in a velvet multiplex chair, tipping my head back, watching as the figures loom larger, much larger, than life—the young, beautiful woman holding the older woman's body to her, weeping over her, feeling everything that is rich and terrible and dark and lonesome in this life, feeling abandoned and full of despair, and beaming it out to us. Beaming it to me. When the actress leans her head back and screams, I draw in a delicate breath and my hands go to my chest. It moves me so much. The tears slide down my cheeks, just as they did in the dream. I sink to my knees and wait for the sirens to come.

ACKNOWLEDGMENTS

I would like to thank . . .

My extraordinary agent, Chris Clemans: champion, coach, advisor, collaborator, and friend.

My brilliant, keen-eyed editor, Valerie Steiker.

The Scribner team: Nan Graham, Roz Lippel, and Colin Harrison, for their early and ongoing support. Thanks also to: Jaya Miceli, Sally Howe, Jennifer Weidman, Kate Lloyd, Kara Watson, Ashley Gilliam, Jason Chappell, and Kyle Kabel.

Agents, assistants, and others at the Clegg Agency: Marion Duvert, Simon Toop, and David Kambhu.

Robert Hass, for his beautiful translation of Yosa Buson's haiku.

My first readers—dear friends—without whom this book (and my life) would be much less interesting: Courtney Brkic, Jessica Cary, Jennifer Firestone, Camille Guthrie, Amelia Kahaney, Jen Lee, Margaret Lewis, Corey Mead, and Idra Novey.

My loving, supportive parents, by blood and by marriage:

ACKNOWLEDGMENTS

Chris and Karen Mead, Joe and Judy Teefey, and Bob and Marcia Sims.

My husband, Corey Mead, and my son, Caleb, for their humor, love, and companionship.

Margaret Lewis, to whom this book is dedicated, for her unfailing, fathoms-deep friendship.

LOOKER

LAURA SIMS

This reading group guide for Looker *includes an introduction, discussion questions, and ideas for enhancing your book club. The suggested questions are intended to help your reading group find new and interesting angles and topics for your discussion. We hope that these ideas will enrich your conversation and increase your enjoyment of the book.*

INTRODUCTION

In this taut, riveting debut, an unhappily childless and recently separated woman becomes fixated on her neighbor—the actress. Though she and the actress live just a few doors apart, a chasm of professional success and personal fulfillment lies between them. The actress, a celebrity with a charmed career, shares a gleaming brownstone with her handsome husband and their three adorable children, while the narrator, working in a dead-end job, lives in a run-down, three-story walk-up with her ex-husband's cat.

After an interaction with the actress at the annual block party takes a disastrous turn, what began as an innocent preoccupation turns into a stunning—and irrevocable—unraveling. Taking up questions of success, celebrity, women's roles, obsession, and privacy, *Looker* deftly reveals the perils of envy.

TOPICS & QUESTIONS
FOR DISCUSSION

1. At the very beginning of the novel, the narrator says that the actress "belongs to us. To our block, I mean" (page 1). Why does she correct herself? How does this set up the narrator's increasingly intense feelings about the actress?

2. The narrator is very familiar with the actress's roles, thinking, for instance, of her breakout in *The Sultan of Hanover Street*, which she watched with Nathan. How does her engagement with the actress's many on-screen roles color her understanding of the actress as a wife, mother, and neighbor?

3. One of the reasons for the dissolution of the narrator's marriage seems to be that the narrator was unable to

conceive a child. How does this impact the narrator's feelings about herself?

4. The narrator teaches her students that Emily Dickinson poems are "full of sex and rage" (page 55). Why are these themes particularly resonant? Are there other ways of interpreting the poems she assigns?

5. When the narrator has lunch with her friend Shana, she at first believes she's getting "appreciative looks" from every man in the room (page 58), but then realizes this might not be the case. How does this shift in reality complicate your understanding of the narrator's reliability? What are other instances of her unreliability?

6. Describe the narrator's transition from tolerating Cat to desperately holding on to her. How does she convince herself that Cat belongs with her?

7. When the narrator feels insecure in front of her students, she wears an outfit that "mirrors the one the actress wore to teach in every single scene of *Working Class*" (page 83). Why? How would you describe the narrator's feelings toward the actress?

8. The narrator fills up the room once intended for her and her husband's child with the actress's discarded

family belongings, making the room into a kind of shrine. How do the narrator's changing feelings about these belongings illuminate her moods?

9. Why do you think the narrator is so fixated on the block party?

10. Why does the narrator engage with Bernardo? Is he the unstable one, or is she?

11. After her months-long obsession with the block party, the narrator's interaction with the actress does not go as expected. Why do you think the narrator, even after the incident with Nathan, chooses to go to the actress's house? What does she hope to get out of the experience?

12. The narrator assigns Elizabeth Bishop's "One Art" to her students (page 141). How does it speak to the way the narrator has responded to losing the things she once had—her job, her marriage, the possibility of a child?

13. On her final day with Cat, why does the narrator make the decision to act as she does? Is it planned or an expression of desperation?

14. The narrator envisions achieving a rapturous closeness with the actress as the novel comes to an end. Are

these just fantasies, or are they more sinister than that?

15. How did you feel after spending so much time in the narrator's head? When you finished reading, did you have sympathy for her? What did you think was going to happen to her afterward?

ENHANCE YOUR BOOK CLUB

1. Read some of the poems the narrator assigns in class: Emily Dickinson's "Wild Nights – Wild Nights!" and "Come slowly – Eden!"; Yosa Buson's "The camellia"; Walt Whitman's "Song of Myself"; John Donne's "Batter my heart, three-person'd God"; Sylvia Plath's "Ariel," "Lady Lazarus," and "Fever 103°"; Wanda Coleman's "American Sonnet (10)"; and Elizabeth Bishop's "One Art." How do these poems deepen your understanding of the novel and the narrator's mind-set?

2. The narrator finds solace—and obsession—in the actress's films. Are there movies or actors you feel particularly connected to? Share them with your group.

3. To read more about Laura Sims and *Looker*, go to https://www.laurasims.net/.